CW01023441

"Rise of the Titan"

Edited by Logan Bruce

Titanic Centenary Edition

Featuring 'Wreck of the Titan' by Morgan Robertson

and assorted short stories and essays

Published by The ORB
www.orb-store.com

Author of Blood of Thrones
"... a breathtaking ride, a very broad canvas ..."
Dr Steve Flanders, School of History, Queen's University Belfast

Profits to Charity pledge

For every copy of this book sold, one pound (20%) of the cover price will go to the charity nominated by Studio NI, the largest Arts and Culture Group in the North of Ireland.

At time of publication, the nominated charity is
Action Cancer (Charity reg no. XN 48533)

Table of Contents

Introduction
By Logan Bruce (Editor)

Morgan Robertson's "The Wreck of the Titan" is a novella that has developed a certain infamy over the years. Summed up, it is a tale set in part aboard the greatest passenger liner ever built, that sets sail on its maiden voyage and encounters an iceberg ...

The infamy of the story comes not from its subject matter, which so closely resembles the facts of the Titanic's maiden voyage in 1912, but the fact that the story was initially published in 1899. Yes, this story apparently predicts the events which came to pass a dozen years later. Surely no coincidence ...

If we are to look at historical coincidences, this is not an isolated incident. Let us compare two other events beloved of fiction writers - the assassinations of Abraham Lincoln and John Fitzgerald Kennedy. American Presidents who lived in troubled times, shot dead in public at the height of their popularity.

Even those facts of the JFK assassination that do not copy the Lincoln killing tend to mirror it. For example, Booth used a pistol and was killed with a rifle, while Oswald used a rifle and was killed with a pistol. Booth shot in a theatre and was cornered in a warehouse, while Oswald shot from a warehouse and was caught in a movie theatre.

A conspiracy theorist might assume that somehow time-travel was involved. Perhaps not in reality, but in a science fiction universe where the laws of physics allowed this. Hence this compilation includes an essay on the links between time-travel and the Titanic.

But why categorise the story as Science Fiction?

"Wreck of the Titan" is Science Fiction in the same way that many near-future stories are: it features scientific or technical aspects that are fictionalised and do not yet exist at the time the story is written.

But unlike his contemporary, Herbert George Wells, the author Morgan Robertson did not follow in the footsteps of Jules Verne by showing how far scientific progress can take the human race. Instead Robertson merely used his story's Science Fiction aspects as a background for the actions of the characters, which is what his story is really about. After all, "Star Wars" is Science Fiction because of its "Flash Gordon" type setting: the story itself is taken largely from Akira Kurosawa's samurai film "The Hidden Fortress".

Morgan Robertson's other works certainly belong in Science Fiction territory. As well as "predicting" the sinking of the Titanic he also wrote of a war in the Pacific ocean, between the United States and the Japanese Empire. Robertson lived to see his work published before he died in 1915 ... thirty years before the Hiroshima bombing avenged the Pearl Harbour attack of 1941.

The Titanic was not the only ship with Ulster links that was lost to ice. The essay 'An Ulsterman among the Icebergs' explains links with Francis Crozier, a polar adventurer of the Victorian age who has been unjustly neglected by history.

The bold and adventurous spirit of Crozier and the men he inspired was best summed up in the poem 'If—' by Rudyard Kipling, and this text would not be complete without its inclusion.

The Titanic was not in unexplored waters, however. She was following a shipping route that had been established centuries before. But exactly who was the first sailor to use that route? Was an Ulsterman responsible for the 'First Crossing of the Atlantic?'

We cannot have a volume about the Titanic which does not devote time to the word "Titan", which has become generic throughout Science Fiction and Fantasy. It is even used in the name of the annual SF & F convention based in Belfast, where the Titanic was built. Hence the inclusion of the essay "Which Titan is TitanCon named after?" ...

And finally, to round out the Titanic theme of the Anthology we have some science to complement the fiction. Specifically, a scientific paper on the molecular bonding that makes mere water in its frozen state hard enough to sink an iron-hulled steamship that weighed over forty thousand tons.

THE WRECK OF THE TITAN

Or, FUTILITY

**BY
MORGAN ROBERTSON**

AUTOGRAPH EDITION
PUBLISHED BY
McCLURE'S MAGAZINE
AND
METROPOLITAN MAGAZINE

Copyright, 1898, by M. F. Mansfield

Copyright, 1912, by Morgan Robertson

**THE QUINN & BODEN CO. PRESS
RAHWAY, N. J.**

**THE WRECK OF THE TITAN;
Or FUTILITY**

THE WRECK OF THE TITAN

CHAPTER I

She was the largest craft afloat and the greatest of the works of men. In her construction and maintenance were involved every science, profession, and trade known to civilization. On her bridge were officers, who, besides being the pick of the Royal Navy, had passed rigid examinations in all studies that pertained to the winds, tides, currents, and geography of the sea; they were not only seamen, but scientists. The same professional standard applied to the personnel of the engine-room, and the steward's department was equal to that of a first-class hotel.

Two brass bands, two orchestras, and a theatrical company entertained the passengers during waking hours; a corps of physicians attended to the temporal, and a corps of chaplains to the spiritual, welfare of all on board, while a well-drilled fire-company soothed the fears of nervous ones and added to the general entertainment by daily practice with their apparatus.

From her lofty bridge ran hidden telegraph lines to the bow, stern engine-room, crow's-nest on the foremast, and to all parts of the ship where work was done, each wire terminating in a marked dial with a movable indicator, containing in its scope every order and answer required in handling the massive hulk, either at the dock or at sea—which eliminated, to a great extent, the hoarse, nerve-racking shouts of officers and sailors.

From the bridge, engine-room, and a dozen places on her deck the ninety-two doors of nineteen water-tight compartments could be closed in half a minute by turning a lever. These doors would also close automatically in the presence of water. With nine compartments flooded the ship would still float, and as no known accident of the sea could possibly fill this many, the steamship *Titan* was considered practically unsinkable.

Built of steel throughout, and for passenger traffic only, she carried no combustible cargo to threaten her destruction by fire; and the immunity from the demand for cargo space had enabled her designers to discard the flat, kettle-bottom of cargo boats and give her the sharp dead-rise—or slant from the keel—of a steam yacht, and this improved her behavior in a seaway. She was eight hundred feet long, of seventy thousand tons' displacement, seventy-five thousand horse-power, and on her trial trip had steamed at a rate of twenty-five knots an hour over the bottom, in the face of unconsidered winds, tides, and currents. In short, she was a floating city—containing within her steel walls all that tends to minimize the dangers and discomforts of the Atlantic voyage—all that makes life enjoyable.

Unsinkable—indestructible, she carried as few boats as would satisfy the laws. These, twenty-four in number, were securely covered and lashed down to their chocks on the upper deck, and if launched would hold five hundred people. She carried no useless, cumbersome life-rafts; but—because the law required it—each of the three thousand berths in the passengers', officers', and crew's quarters contained a cork jacket, while about twenty circular life-buoys were strewn along the rails.

In view of her absolute superiority to other craft, a rule of navigation thoroughly believed in by some captains, but not yet openly followed, was announced by the steamship company to apply to the *Titan*: She would steam at full speed in fog, storm, and sunshine, and on the Northern Lane Route, winter and summer, for the following good and substantial reasons: First, that if another craft should strike her, the force of the impact would be distributed over a larger area if the *Titan* had full headway, and the brunt of the damage would be borne by the other. Second, that if the *Titan* was the aggressor she would certainly destroy the other craft, even at half-speed, and perhaps damage her own bows; while at full speed, she would cut her in two with no more damage to herself than a paintbrush could remedy. In either case, as the lesser of two evils, it was best that the smaller hull should suffer. A third reason was that, at full speed, she could be more easily steered out of danger, and a fourth, that in case of an end-on collision with an iceberg—the only thing afloat that she could not conquer—her bows would be crushed in but a few feet further at full than at half speed, and at the most three compartments would be flooded—which would not matter with six more to spare.

So, it was confidently expected that when her engines had limbered themselves, the steamship *Titan* would land her passengers three thousand miles away with the promptitude and regularity of a railway train. She had beaten all records on her maiden voyage, but, up to the third return trip, had not lowered the time between Sandy Hook and Daunt's Rock to the five-day limit; and it was unofficially rumored among the two thousand passengers who had embarked at New York that an effort would now be made to do so.

CHAPTER II

Eight tugs dragged the great mass to midstream and pointed her nose down the river; then the pilot on the bridge spoke a word or two; the first officer blew a short blast on the whistle and turned a lever; the tugs gathered in their lines and drew off; down in the bowels of the ship three small engines were started, opening the throttles of three large ones; three propellers began to revolve; and the mammoth, with a vibratory tremble running through her great frame, moved slowly to sea.

East of Sandy Hook the pilot was dropped and the real voyage begun. Fifty feet below her deck, in an inferno of noise, and heat, and light, and shadow, coal-passers wheeled the picked fuel from the bunkers to the fire-hold, where half-naked stokers, with faces like those of tortured fiends, tossed it into the eighty white-hot mouths of the furnaces. In the engine-room, oilers passed to and fro, in and out of the plunging, twisting, glistening steel, with oil-cans and waste, overseen by the watchful staff on duty, who listened with strained hearing for a false note in the confused jumble of sound—a clicking of steel out of tune, which would indicate a loosened key or nut. On deck, sailors set the triangular sails on the two masts, to add their propulsion to the momentum of the record-breaker, and the passengers dispersed themselves as suited their several tastes. Some were seated in steamer chairs, well wrapped—for, though it was April, the salt air was chilly—some paced the deck, acquiring their sea legs; others listened to the orchestra in the music-room, or read or wrote in the library, and a few took to their berths—seasick from the slight heave of the ship on the ground-swell.

The decks were cleared, watches set at noon, and then began the never-ending cleaning-up at which steamship sailors put in so much of their time. Headed by a six-foot boatswain, a gang came aft on the starboard side, with paint-buckets and brushes, and distributed themselves along the rail.

"Davits an' stanchions, men—never mind the rail," said the boatswain. "Ladies, better move your chairs back a little. Rowland, climb down out o' that—you'll be overboard. Take a ventilator—no, you'll spill paint—put your bucket away an' get some sandpaper from the yeoman. Work inboard till you get it out o' you."

The sailor addressed—a slight-built man of about thirty, black-bearded and bronzed to the semblance of healthy vigor, but watery-eyed and unsteady of movement—came down from the rail and shambled forward with his bucket. As he reached the group of ladies to whom the boatswain had spoken, his gaze rested on one—a sunny-haired young woman with the blue of the sea in her eyes—who had arisen at his approach. He started, turned aside as if to avoid her, and raising his hand in an embarrassed half-salute, passed on. Out of the boatswain's sight he leaned against the deck-house and panted, while he held his hand to his breast.

"What is it?" he muttered, wearily; "whisky nerves, or the dying flutter of a starved love. Five years, now—and a look from her eyes can stop the blood in my veins—can bring back all the heart-hunger and helplessness, that leads a man to insanity—or this." He looked at his trembling hand, all scarred and tar-stained, passed on forward, and returned with the sandpaper.

The young woman had been equally affected by the meeting. An expression of mingled surprise and terror had come to her pretty, but rather weak face; and without acknowledging his half-salute, she had caught up a little child from the deck behind her, and turning into the saloon door, hurried to the library, where she sank into a chair beside a military-looking gentleman, who glanced up from a book and remarked: "Seen the sea-serpent, Myra, or the Flying Dutchman? What's up?"

"Oh, George—no," she answered in agitated tones. "John Rowland is here—Lieutenant Rowland. I've just seen him—he is so changed—he tried to speak to me."

"Who—that troublesome flame of yours? I never met him, you know, and you haven't told me much about him. What is he—first cabin?"

"No, he seems to be a common sailor; he is working, and is dressed in old clothes—all dirty. And such a dissipated face, too. He seems to have fallen—so low. And it is all since—"

"Since you soured on him? Well, it is no fault of yours, dear. If a man has it in him he'll go to the dogs anyhow. How is his sense of injury? Has he a grievance or a grudge? You're badly upset. What did he say?"

"I don't know—he said nothing—I've always been afraid of him. I've met him three times since then, and he puts such a frightful look in his eyes—and he was so violent, and headstrong, and so terribly angry,—that time. He accused me of leading him on, and playing with him; and he said something about an immutable law of chance, and a governing balance of events—that I couldn't understand, only where he said that for all the suffering we inflict on others, we receive an equal amount ourselves. Then he went away—in such a passion. I've imagined ever since that he would take some revenge—he might steal our Myra—our baby." She strained the smiling child to her breast and went on. "I liked him at first, until I found out that he was an atheist—why, George, he actually denied the existence of God—and to me, a professing Christian."

"He had a wonderful nerve," said the husband, with a smile; "didn't know you very well, I should say."

"He never seemed the same to me after that," she resumed; "I felt as though in the presence of something unclean. Yet I thought how glorious it would be if I could save him to God, and tried to convince him of the loving care of Jesus; but he only ridiculed all I hold sacred, and said, that much as he valued my good opinion, he would not be a hypocrite to gain it, and that he would be honest with himself and others, and express his honest unbelief—the idea; as though one could be honest without God's help—and then, one day, I smelled liquor on his breath—he always smelled of tobacco—and I gave him up. It was then that he—that he broke out."

"Come out and show me this reprobate," said the husband, rising. They went to the door and the young woman peered out. "He is the last man down there—close to the cabin," she said as she drew in. The husband stepped out.

"What! that hang-dog ruffian, scouring the ventilator? So, that's Rowland, of the navy, is it! Well, this is a tumble. Wasn't he broken for conduct unbecoming an officer? Got roaring drunk at the President's levee, didn't he? I think I read of it."

"I know he lost his position and was terribly disgraced," answered the wife.

"Well, Myra, the poor devil is harmless now. We'll be across in a few days, and you needn't meet him on this broad deck. If he hasn't lost all sensibility, he's as embarrassed as you. Better stay in now—it's getting foggy."

CHAPTER III

When the watch turned out at midnight, they found a vicious half-gale blowing from the northeast, which, added to the speed of the steamship, made, so far as effects on her deck went, a fairly uncomfortable whole gale of chilly wind. The head sea, choppy as compared with her great length, dealt the *Titan* successive blows, each one attended by supplementary tremors to the continuous vibrations of the engines—each one sending a cloud of thick spray aloft that reached the crow's-nest on the foremast and battered the pilot-house windows on the bridge in a liquid bombardment that would have broken ordinary glass. A fog-bank, into which the ship had plunged in the afternoon, still enveloped her—damp and impenetrable; and into the gray, ever-receding wall ahead, with two deck officers and three lookouts straining sight and hearing to the utmost, the great racer was charging with undiminished speed.

At a quarter past twelve, two men crawled in from the darkness at the ends of the eighty-foot bridge and shouted to the first officer, who had just taken the deck, the names of the men who had relieved them. Backing up to the pilot-house, the officer repeated the names to a quartermaster within, who entered them in the log-book. Then the men vanished—to their coffee and "watch-below." In a few moments another dripping shape appeared on the bridge and reported the crow's-nest relief.

"Rowland, you say?" bawled the officer above the howling of the wind. "Is he the man who was lifted aboard, drunk, yesterday?"

"Yes, sir."

"Is he still drunk?"

"Yes, sir."

"All right—that'll do. Enter Rowland in the crow's-nest, quartermaster," said the officer; then, making a funnel of his hands, he roared out: "Crow's-nest, there."

"Sir," came the answer, shrill and clear on the gale.

"Keep your eyes open—keep a sharp lookout."

"Very good, sir."

"Been a man-o'-war's-man, I judge, by his answer. They're no good," muttered the officer. He resumed his position at the forward side of the bridge where the wooden railing afforded some shelter from the raw wind, and began the long vigil which would only end when the second officer relieved him, four hours later. Conversation—except in the line of duty—was forbidden among the bridge officers of the *Titan*, and his watchmate, the third officer, stood on the other side of the large bridge binnacle, only leaving this position occasionally to glance in at the compass—which seemed to be his sole duty at sea. Sheltered by one of the deck-houses below, the boatswain and the watch paced back and forth, enjoying the only two hours respite which steamship rules afforded, for the day's work had ended with the going down of the other watch, and at two o'clock the washing of the 'tween-deck would begin, as an opening task in the next day's labor.

By the time one bell had sounded, with its repetition from the crow's-nest, followed by a long-drawn cry—"all's well"—from the lookouts, the last of the two thousand passengers had retired, leaving the spacious cabins and steerage in possession of the watchmen; while, sound asleep in his cabin abaft the chart-room was the captain, the commander who never commanded—unless the ship was in danger; for the pilot had charge, making and leaving port, and the officers, at sea.

Two bells were struck and answered; then three, and the boatswain and his men were lighting up for a final smoke, when there rang out overhead a startling cry from the crow's-nest:

"Something ahead, sir—can't make it out."

The first officer sprang to the engine-room telegraph and grasped the lever. "Sing out what you see," he roared.

"Hard aport, sir—ship on the starboard tack—dead ahead," came the cry.

"Port your wheel—hard over," repeated the first officer to the quartermaster at the helm—who answered and obeyed. Nothing as yet could be seen from the bridge. The powerful steering-engine in the stern ground the rudder over; but before three degrees on the compass card were traversed by the lubber's-point, a seeming thickening of the darkness and fog ahead resolved itself into the square sails of a deep-laden ship, crossing the *Titan's* bow, not half her length away.

"H—l and d—" growled the first officer. "Steady on your course, quartermaster," he shouted. "Stand from under on deck." He turned a lever which closed compartments, pushed a button marked—"Captain's Room," and crouched down, awaiting the crash.

There was hardly a crash. A slight jar shook the forward end of the *Titan* and sliding down her fore-topmast-stay and rattling on deck came a shower of small spars, sails, blocks, and wire rope. Then, in the darkness to starboard and port, two darker shapes shot by—the two halves of the ship she had cut through; and from one of these shapes, where still burned a binnacle light, was heard, high above the confused murmur of shouts and shrieks, a sailorly voice:

"May the curse of God light on you and your cheese-knife, you brass-bound murderers."

The shapes were swallowed in the blackness astern; the cries were hushed by the clamor of the gale, and the steamship *Titan* swung back to her course. The first officer had not turned the lever of the engine-room telegraph.

The boatswain bounded up the steps of the bridge for instructions.

"Put men at the hatches and doors. Send every one who comes on deck to the chart-room. Tell the watchman to notice what the passengers have learned, and clear away that wreck forward as soon as possible." The voice of the officer was hoarse and strained as he gave these directions, and the "aye, aye, sir" of the boatswain was uttered in a gasp.

CHAPTER IV

The crow's-nest "lookout," sixty feet above the deck, had seen every detail of the horror, from the moment when the upper sails of the doomed ship had appeared to him above the fog to the time when the last tangle of wreckage was cut away by his watchmates below. When relieved at four bells, he descended with as little strength in his limbs as was compatible with safety in the rigging. At the rail, the boatswain met him.

"Report your relief, Rowland," he said, "and go into the chart-room!"

On the bridge, as he gave the name of his successor, the first officer seized his hand, pressed it, and repeated the boatswain's order. In the chart-room, he found the captain of the *Titan*, pale-faced and intense in manner, seated at a table, and, grouped around him, the whole of the watch on deck except the officers, lookouts, and quartermasters. The cabin watchmen were there, and some of the watch below, among whom were stokers and coal-passers, and also, a few of the idlers—lampmen, yeomen, and butchers, who, sleeping forward, had been awakened by the terrific blow of the great hollow knife within which they lived.

Three carpenters' mates stood by the door, with sounding-rods in their hands, which they had just shown the captain—dry. Every face, from the captain's down, wore a look of horror and expectancy. A quartermaster followed Rowland in and said:

"Engineer felt no jar in the engine-room, sir; and there's no excitement in the stokehold."

"And you watchmen report no alarm in the cabins. How about the steerage? Is that man back?" asked the captain. Another watchman appeared as he spoke.

"All asleep in the steerage, sir," he said. Then a quartermaster entered with the same report of the forecastles.

"Very well," said the captain, rising; "one by one come into my office—watchmen first, then petty officers, then the men. Quartermasters will watch the door—that no man goes out until I have seen him." He passed into another room, followed by a watchman, who presently emerged and went on deck with a more pleasant expression of face. Another entered and came out; then another, and another, until every man but Rowland had been within the sacred precincts, all to wear the same pleased, or satisfied, look on reappearing. When Rowland entered, the captain, seated at a desk, motioned him to a chair, and asked his name.

"John Rowland," he answered. The captain wrote it down.

"I understand," he said, "that you were in the crow's-nest when this unfortunate collision occurred."

"Yes, sir; and I reported the ship as soon as I saw her."

"You are not here to be censured. You are aware, of course, that nothing could be done, either to avert this terrible calamity, or to save life afterward."

"Nothing at a speed of twenty-five knots an hour in a thick fog, sir." The captain glanced sharply at Rowland and frowned.

"We will not discuss the speed of the ship, my good man," he said, "or the rules of the company. You will find, when you are paid at Liverpool, a package addressed to you at the company's office containing one hundred pounds in banknotes. This, you will receive for your silence in regard to this collision—the reporting of which would embarrass the company and help no one."

"On the contrary, captain, I shall not receive it. On the contrary, sir, I shall speak of this wholesale murder at the first opportunity!"

The captain leaned back and stared at the debauched face, the trembling figure of the sailor, with which this defiant speech so little accorded. Under ordinary circumstances, he would have sent him on deck to be dealt with by the officers. But this was not an ordinary circumstance. In the watery eyes was a look of shock, and horror, and honest indignation; the accents were those of an educated man; and the consequences hanging over himself and the company for which he worked—already complicated by and involved in his efforts to avoid them—which this man might precipitate, were so extreme, that such questions as insolence and difference in rank were not to be thought of. He must meet and subdue this Tartar on common ground—as man to man.

"Are you aware, Rowland," he asked, quietly, "that you will stand alone—that you will be discredited, lose your berth, and make enemies?"

"I am aware of more than that," answered Rowland, excitedly. "I know of the power vested in you as captain. I know that you can order me into irons from this room for any offense you wish to imagine. And I know that an unwitnessed, uncorroborated entry in your official log concerning me would be evidence enough to bring me life imprisonment. But I also know something of admiralty law; that from my prison cell I can send you and your first officer to the gallows."

"You are mistaken in your conceptions of evidence. I could not cause your conviction by a log-book entry; nor could you, from a prison, injure me. What are you, may I ask—an ex-lawyer?"

"A graduate of Annapolis. Your equal in professional technic."

"And you have interest at Washington?"

"None whatever."

"And what is your object in taking this stand—which can do you no possible good, though certainly not the harm you speak of?"

"That I may do one good, strong act in my useless life—that I may help to arouse such a sentiment of anger in the two countries as will forever end this wanton destruction of life and property for the sake of speed—that will save the hundreds of fishing-craft, and others, run down yearly, to their owners, and the crews to their families."

Both men had risen and the captain was pacing the floor as Rowland, with flashing eyes and clinched fists, delivered this declaration.

"A result to be hoped for, Rowland," said the former, pausing before him, "but beyond your power or mine to accomplish. Is the amount I named large enough? Could you fill a position on my bridge?"

"I can fill a higher; and your company is not rich enough to buy me."

"You seem to be a man without ambition; but you must have wants."

"Food, clothing, shelter—and whisky," said Rowland with a bitter, self-contemptuous laugh. The captain reached down a decanter and two glasses from a swinging tray and said as he placed them before him:

"Here is one of your wants; fill up." Rowland's eyes glistened as he poured out a glassful, and the captain followed.

"I will drink with you, Rowland," he said; "here is to our better understanding." He tossed off the liquor; then Rowland, who had waited, said: "I prefer drinking alone, captain," and drank the whisky at a gulp. The captain's face flushed at the affront, but he controlled himself.

"Go on deck, now, Rowland," he said; "I will talk with you again before we reach soundings. Meanwhile, I request—not require, but request—that you hold no useless conversation with your shipmates in regard to this matter."

To the first officer, when relieved at eight bells, the captain said: "He is a broken-down wreck with a temporarily active conscience; but is not the man to buy or intimidate: he knows too much. However, we've found his weak point. If he gets snakes before we dock, his testimony is worthless. Fill him up and I'll see the surgeon, and study up on drugs."

When Rowland turned out to breakfast at seven bells that morning, he found a pint flask in the pocket of his pea-jacket, which he felt of but did not pull out in sight of his watchmates.

"Well, captain," he thought, "you are, in truth, about as puerile, insipid a scoundrel as ever escaped the law. I'll save you your drugged Dutch courage for evidence." But it was not drugged, as he learned later. It was good whisky—a leader—to warm his stomach while the captain was studying.

CHAPTER V

An incident occurred that morning which drew Rowland's thoughts far from the happenings of the night. A few hours of bright sunshine had brought the passengers on deck like bees from a hive, and the two broad promenades resembled, in color and life, the streets of a city. The watch was busy at the inevitable scrubbing, and Rowland, with a swab and bucket, was cleaning the white paint on the starboard taffrail, screened from view by the after deck-house, which shut off a narrow space at the stern. A little girl ran into the inclosure, laughing and screaming, and clung to his legs, while she jumped up and down in an overflow of spirits.

"I wunned 'way," she said; "I wunned 'way from mamma."

Drying his wet hands on his trousers, Rowland lifted the tot and said, tenderly: "Well, little one, you must run back to mamma. You're in bad company." The innocent eyes smiled into his own, and then—a foolish proceeding, which only bachelors are guilty of—he held her above the rail in jesting menace. "Shall I drop you over to the fishes, baby?" he asked, while his features softened to an unwonted smile. The child gave a little scream of fright, and at that instant a young woman appeared around the corner. She sprang toward Rowland like a tigress, snatched the child, stared at him for a moment with dilated eyes, and then disappeared, leaving him limp and nerveless, breathing hard.

"It is her child," he groaned. "That was the mother-look. She is married—married." He resumed his work, with a face as near the color of the paint he was scrubbing as the tanned skin of a sailor may become.

Ten minutes later, the captain, in his office, was listening to a complaint from a very excited man and woman.

"And you say, colonel," said the captain, "that this man Rowland is an old enemy?"

"He is—or was once—a rejected admirer of Mrs. Selfridge. That is all I know of him—except that he has hinted at revenge. My wife is certain of what she saw, and I think the man should be confined."

"Why, captain," said the woman, vehemently, as she hugged her child, "you should have seen him; he was just about to drop Myra over as I seized her—and he had such a frightful leer on his face, too. Oh, it was hideous. I shall not sleep another wink in this ship—I know."

"I beg you will give yourself no uneasiness, madam," said the captain, gravely. "I have already learned something of his antecedents—that he is a disgraced and broken-down naval officer; but, as he has sailed three voyages with us, I had credited his willingness to work before-the-mast to his craving for liquor, which he could not satisfy without money. However—as you think—he may be following you. Was he able to learn of your movements—that you were to take passage in this ship?"

"Why not?" exclaimed the husband; "he must know some of Mrs. Selfridge's friends."

"Yes, yes," she said, eagerly; "I have heard him spoken of, several times."

"Then it is clear," said the captain. "If you will agree, madam, to testify against him in the English courts, I will immediately put him in irons for attempted murder."

"Oh, do, captain," she exclaimed. "I cannot feel safe while he is at liberty. Of course I will testify."

"Whatever you do, captain," said the husband, savagely, "rest assured that I shall put a bullet through his head if he meddles with me or mine again. Then you can put me in irons."

"I will see that he is attended to, colonel," replied the captain as he bowed them out of his office.

But, as a murder charge is not always the best way to discredit a man; and as the captain did not believe that the man who had defied him would murder a child; and as the charge would be difficult to prove in any case, and would cause him much trouble and annoyance, he did not order the arrest of John Rowland, but merely directed that, for the time, he should be kept at work by day in the 'tween-deck, out of sight of the passengers.

Rowland, surprised at his sudden transfer from the disagreeable scrubbing to a "soldier's job" of painting life-buoys in the warm 'tween-deck, was shrewd enough to know that he was being closely watched by the boatswain that morning, but not shrewd enough to affect any symptoms of intoxication or drugging, which might have satisfied his anxious superiors and brought him more whisky. As a result of his brighter eyes and steadier voice—due to the curative sea air—when he turned out for the first dog-watch on deck at four o'clock, the captain and boatswain held an interview in the chart-room, in which the former said: "Do not be alarmed. It is not poison. He is half-way into the horrors now, and this will merely bring them on. He will see snakes, ghosts, goblins, shipwrecks, fire, and all sorts of things. It works in two or three hours. Just drop it into his drinking pot while the port forecastle is empty."

There was a fight in the port forecastle—to which Rowland belonged—at supper-time, which need not be described beyond mention of the fact that Rowland, who was not a participant, had his pot of tea dashed from his hand before he had taken three swallows. He procured a fresh supply and finished his supper; then, taking no part in his watchmates' open discussion of the fight, and guarded discussion of collisions, rolled into his bunk and smoked until eight bells, when he turned out with the rest.

CHAPTER VI

"Rowland," said the big boatswain, as the watch mustered on deck; "take the starboard bridge lookout."

"It is not my trick, boats'n," said Rowland, in surprise.

"Orders from the bridge. Get up there."

Rowland grumbled, as sailors may when aggrieved, and obeyed. The man he relieved reported his name, and disappeared; the first officer sauntered down the bridge, uttered the official, "keep a good lookout," and returned to his post; then the silence and loneliness of a night-watch at sea, intensified by the never-ceasing hum of the engines, and relieved only by the sounds of distant music and laughter from the theater, descended on the forward part of the ship. For the fresh westerly wind, coming with the *Titan*, made nearly a calm on her deck; and the dense fog, though overshone by a bright star-specked sky, was so chilly that the last talkative passenger had fled to the light and life within.

When three bells—half-past nine—had sounded, and Rowland had given in his turn the required call—"all's well"—the first officer left his post and approached him.

"Rowland," he said as he drew near; "I hear you've walked the quarter-deck."

"I cannot imagine how you learned it, sir," replied Rowland; "I am not in the habit of referring to it."

"You told the captain. I suppose the curriculum is as complete at Annapolis as at the Royal Naval College. What do you think of Maury's theories of currents?"

"They seem plausible," said Rowland, unconsciously dropping the "sir"; "but I think that in most particulars he has been proven wrong."

"Yes, I think so myself. Did you ever follow up another idea of his—that of locating the position of ice in a fog by the rate of decrease in temperature as approached?"

"Not to any definite result. But it seems to be only a matter of calculation, and time to calculate. Cold is negative heat, and can be treated like radiant energy, decreasing as the square of the distance."

The officer stood a moment, looking ahead and humming a tune to himself; then, saying: "Yes, that's so," returned to his place.

"Must have a cast-iron stomach," he muttered, as he peered into the binnacle; "or else the boats'n dosed the wrong man's pot."

Rowland glanced after the retreating officer with a cynical smile. "I wonder," he said to himself, "why he comes down here talking navigation to a foremast hand. Why am I up here—out of my turn? Is this something in line with that bottle?" He resumed the short pacing back and forth on the end of the bridge, and the rather gloomy train of thought which the officer had interrupted.

"How long," he mused, "would his ambition and love of profession last him after he had met, and won, and lost, the only woman on earth to him? Why is it—that failure to hold the affections of one among the millions of women who live, and love, can outweigh every blessing in life, and turn a man's nature into a hell, to consume him? Who did she marry? Some one, probably a stranger long after my banishment, who came to her possessed of a few qualities of mind or physique that pleased her,—who did not need to love her—his chances were better without that—and he steps coolly and easily into my heaven. And they tell us, that 'God doeth all things well,' and that there is a heaven where all our unsatisfied wants are attended to—provided we have the necessary faith in it. That means, if it means anything, that after a lifetime of unrecognized allegiance, during which I win nothing but her fear and contempt, I may be rewarded by the love and companionship of her soul. Do I love her soul? Has her soul beauty of face and the figure and carriage of a Venus? Has her soul deep, blue eyes and a sweet, musical voice? Has it wit, and grace, and charm? Has it a wealth of pity for suffering? These are the things I loved. I do not love her soul, if she has one. I do not want it. I want her—I need her." He stopped in his walk and leaned against the bridge railing, with eyes fixed on the fog ahead. He was speaking his thoughts aloud now, and the first officer drew within hearing, listened a moment, and went back. "Working on him," he whispered to the third officer. Then he pushed the button which called the captain, blew a short blast of the steam whistle as a call to the boatswain, and resumed his watch on the drugged lookout, while the third officer conned the ship.

The steam call to the boatswain is so common a sound on a steamship as to generally pass unnoticed. This call affected another besides the boatswain. A little night-gowned figure arose from an under berth in a saloon stateroom, and, with wide-open, staring eyes, groped its way to the deck, unobserved by the watchman. The white, bare little feet felt no cold as they pattered the planks of the deserted promenade, and the little figure had reached the steerage entrance by the time the captain and boatswain had reached the bridge.

"And they talk," went on Rowland, as the three watched and listened; "of the wonderful love and care of a merciful God, who controls all things—who has given me my defects, and my capacity for loving, and then placed Myra Gaunt in my way. Is there mercy to me in this? As part of a great evolutionary principle, which develops the race life at the expense of the individual, it might be consistent with the idea of a God—a first cause. But does the individual who perishes, because unfitted to survive, owe any love, or gratitude to this God? He does not! On the supposition that He exists, I deny it! And on the complete lack of evidence that He does exist, I affirm to myself the integrity of cause and effect—which is enough to explain the Universe, and me. A merciful God—a kind, loving, just, and merciful God—" he burst into a fit of incongruous laughter, which stopped short as he clapped his hands to his stomach and then to his head. "What ails me?" he gasped; "I feel as though I had swallowed hot coals—and my head—and my eyes—I can't see." The pain left him in a moment and the laughter returned. "What's wrong with the starboard anchor? It's moving. It's changing. It's a—what? What on earth is it? On end—and the windlass—and the spare anchors—and the davits—all alive—all moving."

The sight he saw would have been horrid to a healthy mind, but it only moved this man to increased and uncontrollable merriment. The two rails below leading to the stem had arisen before him in a shadowy triangle; and within it were the deck-fittings he had mentioned. The windlass had become a thing of horror, black and forbidding. The two end barrels were the bulging, lightless eyes of a non-descript monster, for which the cable chains had multiplied themselves into innumerable legs and tentacles. And this thing was crawling around within the triangle. The anchor-davits were many-headed serpents which danced on their tails, and the anchors themselves writhed and squirmed in the shape of immense hairy caterpillars, while faces appeared on the two white lantern-towers—grinning and leering at him. With his hands on the bridge rail, and tears streaming down his face, he laughed at the strange sight, but did not speak; and the three, who had quietly approached, drew back to await, while below on the promenade deck, the little white figure, as though attracted by his laughter, turned into the stairway leading to the upper deck.

The phantasmagoria faded to a blank wall of gray fog, and Rowland found sanity to mutter, "They've drugged me"; but in an instant he stood in the darkness of a garden—one that he had known. In the distance were the lights of a house, and close to him was a young girl, who turned from him and fled, even as he called to her.

By a supreme effort of will, he brought himself back to the present, to the bridge he stood upon, and to his duty. "Why must it haunt me through the years?" he groaned; "drunk then—drunk since. She could have saved me, but she chose to damn me." He strove to pace up and down, but staggered, and clung to the rail; while the three watchers approached again, and the little white figure below climbed the upper bridge steps.

"The survival of the fittest," he rambled, as he stared into the fog; "cause and effect. It explains the Universe—and me." He lifted his hand and spoke loudly, as though to some unseen familiar of the deep. "What will be the last effect? Where in the scheme of ultimate balance—under the law of the correlation of energy, will my wasted wealth of love be gathered, and weighed, and credited? What will balance it, and where will I be? Myra,—Myra," he called; "do you know what you have lost? Do you know, in your goodness, and purity, and truth, of what you have done? Do you know—"

The fabric on which he stood was gone, and he seemed to be poised on nothing in a worldless universe of gray—alone. And in the vast, limitless emptiness there was no sound, or life, or change; and in his heart neither fear, nor wonder, nor emotion of any kind, save one—the unspeakable hunger of a love that had failed. Yet it seemed that he was not John Rowland, but some one, or something else; for presently he saw himself, far away—millions of billions of miles; as though on the outermost fringes of the void—and heard his own voice, calling. Faintly, yet distinctly, filled with the concentrated despair of his life, came the call: "Myra,—Myra."

There was an answering call, and looking for the second voice, he beheld her—the woman of his love—on the opposite edge of space; and her eyes held the tenderness, and her voice held the pleading that he had known but in dreams. "Come back," she called; "come back to me." But it seemed that the two could not understand; for again he heard the despairing cry: "Myra, Myra, where are you?" and again the answer: "Come back. Come."

Then in the far distance to the right appeared a faint point of flame, which grew larger. It was approaching, and he dispassionately viewed it; and when he looked again for the two, they were gone, and in their places were two clouds of nebula, which resolved into myriad points of sparkling light and color—whirling, encroaching, until they filled all space. And through them the larger light was coming—and growing larger—straight for him.

He heard a rushing sound, and looking for it, saw in the opposite direction a formless object, as much darker than the gray of the void as the flame was brighter, and it too was growing larger, and coming. And it seemed to him that this light and darkness were the good and evil of his life, and he watched, to see which would reach him first, but felt no surprise or regret when he saw that the darkness was nearest. It came, closer and closer, until it brushed him on the side.

"What have we here, Rowland?" said a voice. Instantly, the whirling points were blotted out; the universe of gray changed to the fog; the flame of light to the moon rising above it, and the shapeless darkness to the form of the first officer. The little white figure, which had just darted past the three watchers, stood at his feet. As though warned by an inner subconsciousness of danger, it had come in its sleep, for safety and care, to its mother's old lover—the strong and the weak—the degraded and disgraced, but exalted—the persecuted, drugged, and all but helpless John Rowland.

With the readiness with which a man who dozes while standing will answer the question that wakens him, he said—though he stammered from the now waning effect of the drug: "Myra's child, sir; it's asleep." He picked up the night gowned little girl, who screamed as she wakened, and folded his pea-jacket around the cold little body.

"Who is Myra?" asked the officer in a bullying tone, in which were also chagrin and disappointment. "You've been asleep yourself."

Before Rowland could reply a shout from the crow's-nest split the air.

"Ice," yelled the lookout; "ice ahead. Iceberg. Right under the bows." The first officer ran amidships, and the captain, who had remained there, sprang to the engine-room telegraph, and this time the lever was turned. But in five seconds the bow of the *Titan* began to lift, and ahead, and on either hand, could be seen, through the fog, a field of ice, which arose in an incline to a hundred feet high in her track. The music in the theater ceased, and among the babel of shouts and cries, and the deafening noise of steel, scraping and crashing over ice, Rowland heard the agonized voice of a woman crying from the bridge steps: "Myra—Myra, where are you? Come back."

CHAPTER VII

Seventy-five thousand tons—dead-weight—rushing through the fog at the rate of fifty feet a second, had hurled itself at an iceberg. Had the impact been received by a perpendicular wall, the elastic resistance of bending plates and frames would have overcome the momentum with no more damage to the passengers than a severe shaking up, and to the ship than the crushing in of her bows and the killing, to a man, of the watch below. She would have backed off, and, slightly down by the head, finished the voyage at reduced speed, to rebuild on insurance money, and benefit, largely, in the end, by the consequent advertising of her indestructibility. But a low beach, possibly formed by the recent overturning of the berg, received the *Titan*, and with her keel cutting the ice like the steel runner of an ice-boat, and her great weight resting on the starboard bilge, she rose out of the sea, higher and higher—until the propellers in the stern were half exposed—then, meeting an easy, spiral rise in the ice under her port bow, she heeled, overbalanced, and crashed down on her side, to starboard.

The holding-down bolts of twelve boilers and three triple-expansion engines, unintended to hold such weights from a perpendicular flooring, snapped, and down through a maze of ladders, gratings, and fore-and-aft bulkheads came these giant masses of steel and iron, puncturing the sides of the ship, even where backed by solid, resisting ice; and filling the engine- and boiler-rooms with scalding steam, which brought a quick, though tortured death, to each of the hundred men on duty in the engineer's department.

Amid the roar of escaping steam, and the bee-like buzzing of nearly three thousand human voices, raised in agonized screams and callings from within the inclosing walls, and the whistling of air through hundreds of open deadlights as the water, entering the holes of the crushed and riven starboard side, expelled it, the *Titan* moved slowly backward and launched herself into the sea, where she floated low on her side—a dying monster, groaning with her death-wound.

A solid, pyramid-like hummock of ice, left to starboard as the steamer ascended, and which projected close alongside the upper, or boat-deck, as she fell over, had caught, in succession, every pair of davits to starboard, bending and wrenching them, smashing boats, and snapping tackles and gripes, until, as the ship cleared herself, it capped the pile of wreckage strewing the ice in front of, and around it, with the end and broken stanchions of the bridge. And in this shattered, box-like structure, dazed by the sweeping fall through an arc of seventy-foot radius, crouched Rowland, bleeding from a cut in his head, and still holding to his breast the little girl—now too frightened to cry.

By an effort of will, he aroused himself and looked. To his eyesight, twisted and fixed to a shorter focus by the drug he had taken, the steamship was little more than a blotch on the moon-whitened fog; yet he thought he could see men clambering and working on the upper davits, and the nearest boat—No. 24—seemed to be swinging by the tackles. Then the fog shut her out, though her position was still indicated by the roaring of steam from her iron lungs. This ceased in time, leaving behind it the horrid humming sound and whistling of air; and when this too was suddenly hushed, and the ensuing silence broken by dull, booming reports—as from bursting compartments—Rowland knew that the holocaust was complete; that the invincible *Titan*, with nearly all of her people, unable to climb vertical floors and ceilings, was beneath the surface of the sea.

Mechanically, his benumbed faculties had received and recorded the impressions of the last few moments; he could not comprehend, to the full, the horror of it all. Yet his mind was keenly alive to the peril of the woman whose appealing voice he had heard and recognized—the woman of his dream, and the mother of the child in his arms. He hastily examined the wreckage. Not a boat was intact. Creeping down to the water's edge, he hailed, with all the power of his weak voice, to possible, but invisible boats beyond the fog—calling on them to come and save the child—to look out for a woman who had been on deck, under the bridge. He shouted this woman's name—the one that he knew—encouraging her to swim, to tread water, to float on wreckage, and to answer him, until he came to her. There was no response, and when his voice had grown hoarse and futile, and his feet numb from the cold of the thawing ice, he returned to the wreckage, weighed down and all but crushed by the blackest desolation that had, so far, come into his unhappy life. The little girl was crying and he tried to soothe her.

"I want mamma," she wailed.

"Hush, baby, hush," he answered, wearily and bitterly; "so do I—more than Heaven, but I think our chances are about even now. Are you cold, little one? We'll go inside, and I'll make a house for us."

He removed his coat, tenderly wrapped the little figure in it, and with the injunction: "Don't be afraid, now," placed her in the corner of the bridge, which rested on its forward side. As he did so, the bottle of whisky fell out of the pocket. It seemed an age since he had found it there, and it required a strong effort of reasoning before he remembered its full significance. Then he raised it, to hurl it down the incline of ice, but stopped himself.

"I'll keep it," he muttered; "it may be safe in small quantities, and we'll need it on this ice." He placed it in a corner; then, removing the canvas cover from one of the wrecked boats, he hung it over the open side and end of the bridge, crawled within, and donned his coat—a ready-made, slop-chest garment, designed for a larger man—and buttoning it around himself and the little girl, lay down on the hard woodwork. She was still crying, but soon, under the influence of the warmth of his body, ceased and went to sleep.

Huddled in a corner, he gave himself up to the torment of his thoughts. Two pictures alternately crowded his mind; one, that of the woman of his dream, entreating him to come back—which his memory clung to as an oracle; the other, of this woman, cold and lifeless, fathoms deep in the sea. He pondered on her chances. She was close to, or on the bridge steps; and boat No. 24, which he was almost sure was being cleared away as he looked, would swing close to her as it descended. She could climb in and be saved—unless the swimmers from doors and hatches should swamp the boat. And, in his agony of mind, he cursed these swimmers, preferring to see her, mentally, the only passenger in the boat, with the watch-on-deck to pull her to safety.

The potent drug he had taken was still at work, and this, with the musical wash of the sea on the icy beach, and the muffled creaking and crackling beneath and around him—the voice of the iceberg—overcame him finally, and he slept, to waken at daylight with limbs stiffened and numb—almost frozen.

And all night, as he slept, a boat with the number twenty-four on her bow, pulled by sturdy sailors and steered by brass-buttoned officers, was making for the Southern Lane—the highway of spring traffic. And, crouched in the stern-sheets of this boat was a moaning, praying woman, who cried and screamed at intervals, for husband and baby, and would not be comforted, even when one of the brass-buttoned officers assured her that her child was safe in the care of John Rowland, a brave and trusty sailor, who was certainly in the other boat with it. He did not tell her, of course, that Rowland had hailed from the berg as she lay unconscious, and that if he still had the child, it was with him there—deserted.

CHAPTER VIII

Rowland, with some misgivings, drank a small quantity of the liquor, and wrapping the still sleeping child in the coat, stepped out on the ice. The fog was gone and a blue, sailless sea stretched out to the horizon. Behind him was ice—a mountain of it. He climbed the elevation and looked at another stretch of vacant view from a precipice a hundred feet high. To his left the ice sloped to a steeper beach than the one behind him, and to the right, a pile of hummocks and taller peaks, interspersed with numerous cañons and caves, and glistening with waterfalls, shut out the horizon in this direction. Nowhere was there a sail or steamer's smoke to cheer him, and he retraced his steps. When but half-way to the wreckage, he saw a moving white object approaching from the direction of the peaks.

His eyes were not yet in good condition, and after an uncertain scrutiny he started at a run; for he saw that the mysterious white object was nearer the bridge than himself, and rapidly lessening the distance. A hundred yards away, his heart bounded and the blood in his veins felt cold as the ice under foot, for the white object proved to be a traveler from the frozen North, lean and famished—a polar bear, who had scented food and was seeking it—coming on at a lumbering run, with great red jaws half open and yellow fangs exposed. Rowland had no weapon but a strong jackknife, but this he pulled from his pocket and opened as he ran. Not for an instant did he hesitate at a conflict that promised almost certain death; for the presence of this bear involved the safety of a child whose life had become of more importance to him than his own. To his horror, he saw it creep out of the opening in its white covering, just as the bear turned the corner of the bridge.

"Go back, baby, go back," he shouted, as he bounded down the slope. The bear reached the child first, and with seemingly no effort, dashed it, with a blow of its massive paw, a dozen feet away, where it lay quiet. Turning to follow, the brute was met by Rowland.

The bear rose to his haunches, sank down, and charged; and Rowland felt the bones of his left arm crushing under the bite of the big, yellow-fanged jaws. But, falling, he buried the knife-blade in the shaggy hide, and the bear, with an angry snarl, spat out the mangled member and dealt him a sweeping blow which sent him farther along the ice than the child had gone. He arose, with broken ribs, and—scarcely feeling the pain—awaited the second charge. Again was the crushed and useless arm gripped in the yellow vise, and again was he pressed backward; but this time he used the knife with method. The great snout was pressing his breast; the hot, fetid breath was in his nostrils; and at his shoulder the hungry eyes were glaring into his own. He struck for the left eye of the brute and struck true. The five-inch blade went in to the handle, piercing the brain, and the animal, with a convulsive spring which carried him half-way to his feet by the wounded arm, reared up, with paws outstretched, to full eight feet of length, then sagged down, and with a few spasmodic kicks, lay still. Rowland had done what no Innuit hunter will attempt—he had fought and killed the Tiger-of-the-North with a knife.

It had all happened in a minute, but in that minute he was crippled for life; for in the quiet of a hospital, the best of surgical skill could hardly avail to reset the fractured particles of bone in the limp arm, and bring to place the crushed ribs. And he was adrift on a floating island of ice, with the temperature near the freezing point, and without even the rude appliances of the savage.

He painfully made his way to the little pile of red and white, and lifted it with his uninjured arm, though the stooping caused him excruciating torture. The child was bleeding from four deep, cruel scratches, extending diagonally from the right shoulder down the back; but he found upon examination that the soft, yielding bones were unbroken, and that her unconsciousness came from the rough contact of the little forehead with the ice; for a large lump had raised.

Of pure necessity, his first efforts must be made in his own behalf; so wrapping the baby in his coat he placed it in his shelter, and cut and made from the canvas a sling for his dangling arm. Then, with knife, fingers, and teeth, he partly skinned the bear—often compelled to pause to save himself from fainting with pain—and cut from the warm but not very thick layer of fat a broad slab, which, after bathing the wounds at a near-by pool, he bound firmly to the little one's back, using the torn night-gown for a bandage.

He cut the flannel lining from his coat, and from that of the sleeves made nether garments for the little limbs, doubling the surplus length over the ankles and tying in place with rope-yarns from a boat-lacing. The body lining he wrapped around her waist, inclosing the arms, and around the whole he passed turn upon turn of canvas in strips, marling the mummy-like bundle with yarns, much as a sailor secures chafing-gear to the doubled parts of a hawser—a process when complete, that would have aroused the indignation of any mother who saw it. But he was only a man, and suffering mental and physical anguish.

By the time he had finished, the child had recovered consciousness, and was protesting its misery in a feeble, wailing cry. But he dared not stop—to become stiffened with cold and pain. There was plenty of fresh water from melting ice, scattered in pools. The bear would furnish food; but they needed fire, to cook this food, keep them warm, and the dangerous inflammation from their hurts, and to raise a smoke to be seen by passing craft.

He recklessly drank from the bottle, needing the stimulant, and reasoning, perhaps rightly, that no ordinary drug could affect him in his present condition; then he examined the wreckage—most of it good kindling wood. Partly above, partly below the pile, was a steel lifeboat, decked over air-tight ends, now doubled to more than a right angle and resting on its side. With canvas hung over one half, and a small fire in the other, it promised, by its conducting property, a warmer and better shelter than the bridge. A sailor without matches is an anomaly. He whittled shavings, kindled the fire, hung the canvas and brought the child, who begged piteously for a drink of water.

He found a tin can—possibly left in a leaky boat before its final hoist to the davits—and gave her a drink, to which he had added a few drops of the whisky. Then he thought of breakfast. Cutting a steak from the hindquarters of the bear, he toasted it on the end of a splinter and found it sweet and satisfying; but when he attempted to feed the child, he understood the necessity of freeing its arms—which he did, sacrificing his left shirtsleeve to cover them. The change and the food stopped its crying for a while, and Rowland lay down with it in the warm boat. Before the day had passed the whisky was gone and he was delirious with fever, while the child was but little better.

CHAPTER IX

With lucid intervals, during which he replenished or rebuilt the fire, cooked the bear-meat, and fed and dressed the wounds of the child, this delirium lasted three days. His suffering was intense. His arm, the seat of throbbing pain, had swollen to twice the natural size, while his side prevented him taking a full breath, voluntarily. He had paid no attention to his own hurts, and it was either the vigor of a constitution that years of dissipation had not impaired, or some anti-febrile property of bear-meat, or the absence of the exciting whisky that won the battle. He rekindled the fire with his last match on the evening of the third day and looked around the darkening horizon, sane, but feeble in body and mind.

If a sail had appeared in the interim, he had not seen it; nor was there one in sight now. Too weak to climb the slope, he returned to the boat, where the child, exhausted from fruitless crying, was now sleeping. His unskillful and rather heroic manner of wrapping it up to protect it from cold had, no doubt, contributed largely to the closing of its wounds by forcibly keeping it still, though it must have added to its present sufferings. He looked for a moment on the wan, tear-stained little face, with its fringe of tangled curls peeping above the wrappings of canvas, and stooping painfully down, kissed it softly; but the kiss awakened it and it cried for its mother. He could not soothe it, nor could he try; and with a formless, wordless curse against destiny welling up from his heart, he left it and sat down on the wreckage at some distance away.

"We'll very likely get well," he mused, gloomily, "unless I let the fire go out. What then? We can't last longer than the berg, and not much longer than the bear. We must be out of the tracks—we were about nine hundred miles out when we struck; and the current sticks to the fog-belt here—about west-sou'west—but that's the surface water. These deep fellows have currents of their own. There's no fog; we must be to the southward of the belt—between the Lanes. They'll run their boats in the other Lane after this, I think—the money-grabbing wretches. Curse them—if they've drowned her. Curse them, with their water-tight compartments, and their logging of the lookouts. Twenty-four boats for three thousand people lashed down with tarred gripe-lashings—thirty men to clear them away, and not an axe on the boat-deck or a sheath-knife on a man. Could she have got away? If they got that boat down, they might have taken her in from the steps; and the mate knew I had her child—he would tell her. Her name must be Myra, too; it was her voice I heard in that dream. That was hasheesh. What did they drug me for? But the whisky was all right. It's all done with now, unless I get ashore—but will I?"

The moon rose above the castellated structure to the left, flooding the icy beach with ashen-gray light, sparkling in a thousand points from the cascades, streams, and rippling pools, throwing into blackest shadow the gullies and hollows, and bringing to his mind, in spite of the weird beauty of the scene, a crushing sense of loneliness—of littleness—as though the vast pile of inorganic desolation which held him was of far greater importance than himself, and all the hopes, plans, and fears of his lifetime. The child had cried itself to sleep again, and he paced up and down the ice.

"Up there," he said, moodily, looking into the sky, where a few stars shone faintly in the flood from the moon; "Up there—somewhere—they don't know just where—but somewhere up above, is the Christians' Heaven. Up there is their good God—who has placed Myra's child here—their good God whom they borrowed from the savage, bloodthirsty race that invented him. And down below us—somewhere again—is their hell and their bad god, whom they invented themselves. And they give us our choice—Heaven or hell. It is not so—not so. The great mystery is not solved—the human heart is not helped in this way. No good, merciful God created this world or its conditions. Whatever may be the nature of the causes at work beyond our mental vision, one fact is indubitably proven—that the qualities of mercy, goodness, justice, play no part in the governing scheme. And yet, they say the core of all religions on earth is the belief in this. Is it? Or is it the cowardly, human fear of the unknown—that impels the savage mother to throw her babe to a crocodile—that impels the civilized man to endow churches—that has kept in existence from the beginning a class of soothsayers, medicine-men, priests, and clergymen, all living on the hopes and fears excited by themselves?

"And people pray—millions of them—and claim they are answered. Are they? Was ever supplication sent into that sky by troubled humanity answered, or even heard? Who knows? They pray for rain and sunshine, and both come in time. They pray for health and success and both are but natural in the marching of events. This is not evidence. But they say that they know, by spiritual uplifting, that they are heard, and comforted, and answered at the moment. Is not this a physiological experiment? Would they not feel equally tranquil if they repeated the multiplication table, or boxed the compass?

"Millions have believed this—that prayers are answered—and these millions have prayed to different gods. Were they all wrong or all right? Would a tentative prayer be listened to? Admitting that the Bibles, and Korans, and Vedas, are misleading and unreliable, may there not be an unseen, unknown Being, who knows my heart—who is watching me now? If so, this Being gave me my reason, which doubts Him, and on Him is the responsibility. And would this being, if he exists, overlook a defect for which I am not to blame, and listen to a prayer from me, based on the mere chance that I might be mistaken? Can an unbeliever, in the full strength of his reasoning powers, come to such trouble that he can no longer stand alone, but must cry for help to an imagined power? Can such time come to a sane man—to me?" He looked at the dark line of vacant horizon. It was seven miles away; New York was nine hundred; the moon in the east over two hundred thousand, and the stars above, any number of billions. He was alone, with a sleeping child, a dead bear, and the Unknown. He walked softly to the boat and looked at the little one for a moment; then, raising his head, he whispered: "For you, Myra."

Sinking to his knees the atheist lifted his eyes to the heavens, and with his feeble voice and the fervor born of helplessness, prayed to the God that he denied. He begged for the life of the waif in his care—for the safety of the mother, so needful to the little one—and for courage and strength to do his part and bring them together. But beyond the appeal for help in the service of others, not one word or expressed thought of his prayer included himself as a beneficiary. So much for pride. As he rose to his feet, the flying-jib of a bark appeared around the corner of ice to the right of the beach, and a moment later the whole moon-lit fabric came into view, wafted along by the faint westerly air, not half a mile away.

He sprang to the fire, forgetting his pain, and throwing on wood, made a blaze. He hailed, in a frenzy of excitement: "Bark ahoy! Bark ahoy! Take us off," and a deep-toned answer came across the water.

"Wake up, Myra," he cried, as he lifted the child; "wake up. We're going away."

"We goin' to mamma?" she asked, with no symptoms of crying.

"Yes, we're going to mamma, now—that is," he added to himself; "if that clause in the prayer is considered."

Fifteen minutes later as he watched the approach of a white quarter-boat, he muttered: "That bark was there—half a mile back in this wind—before I thought of praying. Is that prayer answered? Is she safe?"

CHAPTER X

On the first floor of the London Royal Exchange is a large apartment studded with desks, around and between which surges a hurrying, shouting crowd of brokers, clerks, and messengers. Fringing this apartment are doors and hallways leading to adjacent rooms and offices, and scattered through it are bulletin-boards, on which are daily written in duplicate the marine casualties of the world. At one end is a raised platform, sacred to the presence of an important functionary. In the technical language of the "City," the apartment is known as the "Room," and the functionary, as the "Caller," whose business it is to call out in a mighty sing-song voice the names of members wanted at the door, and the bare particulars of bulletin news prior to its being chalked out for reading.

It is the headquarters of Lloyds—the immense association of underwriters, brokers, and shipping-men, which, beginning with the customers at Edward Lloyd's coffee-house in the latter part of the seventeenth century, has, retaining his name for a title, developed into a corporation so well equipped, so splendidly organized and powerful, that kings and ministers of state appeal to it at times for foreign news.

Not a master or mate sails under the English flag but whose record, even to forecastle fights, is tabulated at Lloyds for the inspection of prospective employers. Not a ship is cast away on any inhabitable coast of the world, during underwriters' business hours, but what that mighty sing-song cry announces the event at Lloyds within thirty minutes.

One of the adjoining rooms is known as the Chart-room. Here can be found in perfect order and sequence, each on its roller, the newest charts of all nations, with a library of nautical literature describing to the last detail the harbors, lights, rocks, shoals, and sailing directions of every coast-line shown on the charts; the tracks of latest storms; the changes of ocean currents, and the whereabouts of derelicts and icebergs. A member at Lloyds acquires in time a theoretical knowledge of the sea seldom exceeded by the men who navigate it.

Another apartment—the Captain's room—is given over to joy and refreshment, and still another, the antithesis of the last, is the

Intelligence office, where anxious ones inquire for and are told the latest news of this or that overdue ship.

On the day when the assembled throng of underwriters and brokers had been thrown into an uproarious panic by the Crier's announcement that the great *Titan* was destroyed, and the papers of Europe and America were issuing extras giving the meager details of the arrival at New York of one boat-load of her people, this office had been crowded with weeping women and worrying men, who would ask, and remain to ask again, for more news. And when it came—a later cablegram,—giving the story of the wreck and the names of the captain, first officer, boatswain, seven sailors, and one lady passenger as those of the saved, a feeble old gentleman had raised his voice in a quavering scream, high above the sobbing of women, and said:

"My daughter-in-law is safe; but where is my son,—where is my son, and my grandchild?" Then he had hurried away, but was back again the next day, and the next. And when, on the tenth day of waiting and watching, he learned of another boat-load of sailors and children arrived at Gibraltar, he shook his head, slowly, muttering: "George, George," and left the room. That night, after telegraphing the consul at Gibraltar of his coming, he crossed the channel.

In the first tumultuous riot of inquiry, when underwriters had climbed over desks and each other to hear again of the wreck of the *Titan*, one—the noisiest of all, a corpulent, hook-nosed man with flashing black eyes—had broken away from the crowd and made his way to the Captain's room, where, after a draught of brandy, he had seated himself heavily, with a groan that came from his soul.

"Father Abraham," he muttered; "this will ruin me."

Others came in, some to drink, some to condole—all, to talk.

"Hard hit, Meyer?" asked one.

"Ten thousand," he answered, gloomily.

"Serve you right," said another, unkindly; "have more baskets for your eggs. Knew you'd bring up."

Though Mr. Meyer's eyes sparkled at this, he said nothing, but drank himself stupid and was assisted home by one of his clerks. From this on, neglecting his business—excepting to occasionally visit the bulletins—he spent his time in the Captain's room drinking heavily, and bemoaning his luck. On the tenth day he read with watery eyes, posted on the bulletin below the news of the arrival at Gibraltar of the second boat-load of people, the following:

"Life-buoy of *Royal Age*, London, picked up among wreckage in Lat. 45-20, N. Lon. 54-31, W. Ship *Arctic*, Boston, Capt. Brandt."

"Oh, mine good God," he howled, as he rushed toward the Captain's room.

"Poor devil—poor damn fool of an Israelite," said one observer to another. "He covered the whole of the *Royal Age*, and the biggest chunk of the *Titan*. It'll take his wife's diamonds to settle."

Three weeks later, Mr. Meyer was aroused from a brooding lethargy, by a crowd of shouting underwriters, who rushed into the Captain's room, seized him by the shoulders, and hurried him out and up to a bulletin.

"Read it, Meyer—read it. What d'you think of it?" With some difficulty he read aloud, while they watched his face:

"John Rowland, sailor of the *Titan*, with child passenger, name unknown, on board *Peerless*, Bath, at Christiansand, Norway. Both dangerously ill. Rowland speaks of ship cut in half night before loss of *Titan*."

"What do you make of it, Meyer—*Royal Age*, isn't it?" asked one.

"Yes," vociferated another, "I've figured back. Only ship not reported lately. Overdue two months. Was spoken same day fifty miles east of that iceberg."

"Sure thing," said others. "Nothing said about it in the captain's statement—looks queer."

"Vell, vwhat of it," said Mr. Meyer, painfully and stupidly: "dere is a collision clause in der *Titan's* policy; I merely bay the money to der steamship company instead of to der *Royal Age* beeple."

"But why did the captain conceal it?" they shouted at him. "What's his object—assured against collision suits?"

"Der looks of it, berhaps—looks pad."

"Nonsense, Meyer, what's the matter with you? Which one of the lost tribes did you spring from—you're like none of your race—drinking yourself stupid like a good Christian. I've got a thousand on the *Titan*, and if I'm to pay it I want to know why. You've got the heaviest risk and the brain to fight for it—you've got to do it. Go home, straighten up, and attend to this. We'll watch Rowland till you take hold. We're all caught."

They put him into a cab, took him to a Turkish bath, and then home.

The next morning he was at his desk, clear-eyed and clear-headed, and for a few weeks was a busy, scheming man of business.

CHAPTER XI

On a certain morning, about two months after the announcement of the loss of the *Titan*, Mr. Meyer sat at his desk in the Rooms, busily writing, when the old gentleman who had bewailed the death of his son in the Intelligence office tottered in and took a chair beside him.

"Good morning, Mr. Selfridge," he said, scarcely looking up; "I suppose you have come to see der insurance paid over. Der sixty days are up."

"Yes, yes, Mr. Meyer," said the old gentleman, wearily; "of course, as merely a stockholder, I can take no active part; but I am a member here, and naturally a little anxious. All I had in the world—even to my son and grandchild—was in the *Titan*."

"It is very sad, Mr. Selfridge; you have my deepest sympathy. I pelieve you are der largest holder of *Titan* stock—about one hundred thousand, is it not?"

"About that."

"I am der heaviest insurer; so Mr. Selfridge, this battle will be largely petween you and myself."

"Battle—is there to be any difficulty?" asked Mr. Selfridge, anxiously.

"Berhaps—I do not know. Der underwriters and outside companies have blaced matters in my hands and will not bay until I take der initiative. We must hear from one John Rowland, who, with a little child, was rescued from der berg and taken to Christiansand. He has been too sick to leave der ship which found him and is coming up der Thames in her this morning. I have a carriage at der dock and expect him at my office py noon. Dere is where we will dransact this little pizness—not here."

"A child—saved," queried the old gentleman; "dear me, it may be little Myra. She was not at Gibraltar with the others. I would not care—I would not care much about the money, if she was safe. But my son—my only son—is gone; and, Mr. Meyer, I am a ruined man if this insurance is not paid."

"And I am a ruined man if it is," said Mr. Meyer, rising. "Will you come around to der office, Mr. Selfridge? I expect der attorney and Captain Bryce are dere now." Mr. Selfridge arose and accompanied him to the street.

A rather meagerly-furnished private office in Threadneedle Street, partitioned off from a larger one bearing Mr. Meyer's name in the window, received the two men, one of whom, in the interests of good business, was soon to be impoverished. They had not waited a minute before Captain Bryce and Mr. Austen were announced and ushered in. Sleek, well-fed, and gentlemanly in manner, perfect types of the British naval officer, they bowed politely to Mr. Selfridge when Mr. Meyer introduced them as the captain and first officer of the *Titan*, and seated themselves. A few moments later brought a shrewd-looking person whom Mr. Meyer addressed as the attorney for the steamship company, but did not introduce; for such are the amenities of the English system of caste.

"Now then, gentlemen," said Mr. Meyer, "I pelieve we can broceed to pizness up to a certain point—berhaps further. Mr. Thompson, you have the affidavit of Captain Bryce?"

"I have," said the attorney, producing a document which Mr. Meyer glanced at and handed back.

"And in this statement, captain," he said, "you have sworn that der voyage was uneventful up to der moment of der wreck—that is," he added, with an oily smile, as he noticed the paling of the captain's face—"that nothing occurred to make der *Titan* less seaworthy or manageable?"

"That is what I swore to," said the captain, with a little sigh.

"You are part owner, are you not, Captain Bryce?"

"I own five shares of the company's stock."

"I have examined der charter and der company lists," said Mr. Meyer; "each boat of der company is, so far as assessments and dividends are concerned, a separate company. I find you are listed as owning two sixty-seconds of der *Titan* stock. This makes you, under der law, part owner of der *Titan*, and responsible as such."

"What do you mean, sir, by that word responsible?" said Captain Bryce, quickly.

For answer, Mr. Meyer elevated his black eyebrows, assumed an attitude of listening, looked at his watch and went to the door, which, as he opened, admitted the sound of carriage wheels.

"In here," he called to his clerks, then faced the captain.

"What do I mean, Captain Bryce?" he thundered. "I mean that you have concealed in your sworn statement all reference to der fact that you collided with and sunk the ship *Royal Age* on der night before the wreck of your own ship."

"Who says so—how do you know it?" blustered the captain. "You have only that bulletin statement of the man Rowland—an irresponsible drunkard."

"The man was lifted aboard drunk at New York," broke in the first officer, "and remained in a condition of delirium tremens up to the shipwreck. We did not meet the *Royal Age* and are in no way responsible for her loss."

"Yes," added Captain Bryce, "and a man in that condition is liable to see anything. We listened to his ravings on the night of the wreck. He was on lookout—on the bridge. Mr. Austen, the boats'n, and myself were close to him."

Before Mr. Meyer's oily smile had indicated to the flustered captain that he had said too much, the door opened and admitted Rowland, pale, and weak, with empty left sleeve, leaning on the arm of a bronze-bearded and manly-looking giant who carried little Myra on the other shoulder, and who said, in the breezy tone of the quarter-deck:

"Well, I've brought him, half dead; but why couldn't you give me time to dock my ship? A mate can't do everything."

"And this is Captain Barry, of der *Peerless*," said Mr. Meyer, taking his hand. "It is all right, my friend; you will not lose. And this is Mr. Rowland—and this is der little child. Sit down, my friend. I congratulate you on your escape."

"Thank you," said Rowland, weakly, as he seated himself; "they cut my arm off at Christiansand, and I still live. That is my escape."

Captain Bryce and Mr. Austen, pale and motionless, stared hard at this man, in whose emaciated face, refined by suffering to the almost spiritual softness of age, they hardly recognized the features of the troublesome sailor of the *Titan*. His clothing, though clean, was ragged and patched.

Mr. Selfridge had arisen and was also staring, not at Rowland, but at the child, who, seated in the lap of the big Captain Barry, was looking around with wondering eyes. Her costume was unique. A dress of bagging-stuff, put together—as were her canvas shoes and hat—with sail-twine in sail-makers' stitches, three to the inch, covered skirts and underclothing made from old flannel shirts. It represented many an hour's work of the watch-below, lovingly bestowed by the crew of the *Peerless*; for the crippled Rowland could not sew. Mr. Selfridge approached, scanned the pretty features closely, and asked:

"What is her name?"

"Her first name is Myra," answered Rowland. "She remembers that; but I have not learned her last name, though I knew her mother years ago—before her marriage."

"Myra, Myra," repeated the old gentleman; "do you know me? Don't you know me?" He trembled visibly as he stooped and kissed her. The little forehead puckered and wrinkled as the child struggled with memory; then it cleared and the whole face sweetened to a smile.

"Gwampa," she said.

"Oh, God, I thank thee," murmured Mr. Selfridge, taking her in his arms. "I have lost my son, but I have found his child—my granddaughter."

"But, sir," asked Rowland, eagerly; "you—this child's grandfather? Your son is lost, you say? Was he on board the *Titan*? And the mother—was she saved, or is she, too—" he stopped unable to continue.

"The mother is safe—in New York; but the father, my son, has not yet been heard from," said the old man, mournfully.

Rowland's head sank and he hid his face for a moment in his arm, on the table at which he sat. It had been a face as old, and worn, and weary as that of the white-haired man confronting him. On it, when it raised—flushed, bright-eyed and smiling—was the glory of youth.

"I trust, sir," he said, "that you will telegraph her. I am penniless at present, and, besides, do not know her name."

"Selfridge—which, of course, is my own name. Mrs. Colonel, or Mrs. George Selfridge. Our New York address is well known. But I shall cable her at once; and, believe me, sir, although I can understand that our debt to you cannot be named in terms of money, you need not be penniless long. You are evidently a capable man, and I have wealth and influence."

Rowland merely bowed, slightly, but Mr. Meyer muttered to himself: "Vealth and influence. Berhaps not. Now, gentlemen," he added, in a louder tone, "to pizness. Mr. Rowland, will you tell us about der running down of der *Royal Age*?"

"Was it the *Royal Age*?" asked Rowland. "I sailed in her one voyage. Yes, certainly."

Mr. Selfridge, more interested in Myra than in the coming account, carried her over to a chair in the corner and sat down, where he fondled and talked to her after the manner of grandfathers the world over, and Rowland, first looking steadily into the faces of the two men he had come to expose, and whose presence he had thus far ignored, told, while they held their teeth tight together and often buried their finger-nails in their palms, the terrible story of the cutting in half of the ship on the first night out from New York, finishing with the attempted bribery and his refusal.

"Vell, gentlemen, vwhat do you think of that?" asked Mr. Meyer, looking around.

"A lie, from beginning to end," stormed Captain Bryce.

Rowland rose to his feet, but was pressed back by the big man who had accompanied him—who then faced Captain Bryce and said, quietly:

"I saw a polar bear that this man killed in open fight. I saw his arm afterward, and while nursing him away from death I heard no whines or complaints. He can fight his own battles when well, and when sick I'll do it for him. If you insult him again in my presence I'll knock your teeth down your throat."

CHAPTER XII

There was a moment's silence while the two captains eyed one another, broken by the attorney, who said:

"Whether this story is true or false, it certainly has no bearing on the validity of the policy. If this happened, it was after the policy attached and before the wreck of the *Titan*."

"But der concealment—der concealment," shouted Mr. Meyer, excitedly.

"Has no bearing, either. If he concealed anything it was done after the wreck, and after your liability was confirmed. It was not even barratry. You must pay this insurance."

"I will not bay it. I will not. I will fight you in der courts." Mr. Meyer stamped up and down the floor in his excitement, then stopped with a triumphant smile, and shook his finger into the face of the attorney.

"And even if der concealment will not vitiate der policy, der fact that he had a drunken man on lookout when der *Titan* struck der iceberg will be enough. Go ahead and sue. I will not pay. He was part owner."

"You have no witnesses to that admission," said the attorney. Mr. Meyer looked around the group and the smile left his face.

"Captain Bryce was mistaken," said Mr. Austen. "This man was drunk at New York, like others of the crew. But he was sober and competent when on lookout. I discussed theories of navigation with him during his trick on the bridge that night and he spoke intelligently."

"But you yourself said, not ten minutes ago, that this man was in a state of delirium tremens up to der collision," said Mr. Meyer.

"What I said and what I will admit under oath are two different things," said the officer, desperately. "I may have said anything under the excitement of the moment—when we were accused of such an infamous crime. I say now, that John Rowland, whatever may have been his condition on the preceding night, was a sober and competent lookout at the time of the wreck of the *Titan*."

"Thank you," said Rowland, dryly, to the first officer; then, looking into the appealing face of Mr. Meyer, he said:

"I do not think it will be necessary to brand me before the world as an inebriate in order to punish the company and these men. Barratry, as I understand it, is the unlawful act of a captain or crew at sea, causing damage or loss; and it only applies when the parties are purely employees. Did I understand rightly—that Captain Bryce was part owner of the *Titan*?"

"Yes," said Mr. Meyer, "he owns stock; and we insure against barratry; but this man, as part owner, could not fall back on it."

"And an unlawful act," went on Rowland, "perpetrated by a captain who is part owner, which might cause shipwreck, and, during the perpetration of which shipwreck really occurs, will be sufficient to void the policy."

"Certainly," said Mr. Meyer, eagerly. "You were drunk on der lookout—you were raving drunk, as he said himself. You will swear to this, will you not, my friend? It is bad faith with der underwriters. It annuls der insurance. You admit this, Mr. Thompson, do you not?"

"That is law," said the attorney, coldly.

"Was Mr. Austen a part owner, also?" asked Rowland, ignoring Mr. Meyer's view of the case.

"One share, is it not, Mr. Austen?" asked Mr. Meyer, while he rubbed his hands and smiled. Mr. Austen made no sign of denial and Rowland continued:

"Then, for drugging a sailor into a stupor, and having him on lookout out of his turn while in that condition, and at the moment when the *Titan* struck the iceberg, Captain Bryce and Mr. Austen have, as part owners, committed an act which nullifies the insurance on that ship."

"You infernal, lying scoundrel!" roared Captain Bryce. He strode toward Rowland with threatening face. Half-way, he was stopped by the impact of a huge brown fist which sent him reeling and staggering across the room toward Mr. Selfridge and the child, over whom he floundered to the floor—a disheveled heap,—while the big Captain Barry examined teeth-marks on his knuckles, and every one else sprang to their feet.

"I told you to look out," said Captain Barry. "Treat my friend respectfully." He glared steadily at the first officer, as though inviting him to duplicate the offense; but that gentleman backed away from him and assisted the dazed Captain Bryce to a chair, where he felt of his loosened teeth, spat blood upon Mr. Meyer's floor, and gradually awakened to a realization of the fact that he had been knocked down—and by an American.

Little Myra, unhurt but badly frightened, began to cry and call for Rowland in her own way, to the wonder, and somewhat to the scandal of the gentle old man who was endeavoring to soothe her.

"Dammy," she cried, as she struggled to go to him; "I want Dammy—Dammy—Da-a-may."

"Oh, what a pad little girl," said the jocular Mr. Meyer, looking down on her. "Where did you learn such language?"

"It is my nickname," said Rowland, smiling in spite of himself. "She has coined the word," he explained to the agitated Mr. Selfridge, who had not yet comprehended what had happened; "and I have not yet been able to persuade her to drop it—and I could not be harsh with her. Let me take her, sir." He seated himself, with the child, who nestled up to him contentedly and soon was tranquil.

"Now, my friend," said Mr. Meyer, "you must tell us about this drugging." Then while Captain Bryce, under the memory of the blow he had received, nursed himself into an insane fury; and Mr. Austen, with his hand resting lightly on the captain's shoulder ready to restrain him, listened to the story; and the attorney drew up a chair and took notes of the story; and Mr. Selfridge drew his chair close to Myra and paid no attention to the story at all, Rowland recited the events prior to and succeeding the shipwreck. Beginning with the finding of the whisky in his pocket, he told of his being called to the starboard bridge lookout in place of the rightful incumbent; of the sudden and strange interest Mr. Austen displayed as to his knowledge of navigation; of the pain in his stomach, the frightful shapes he had seen on the deck beneath and the sensations of his dream—leaving out only the part which bore on the woman he loved; he told of the sleep-walking child which awakened him, of the crash of ice and instant wreck, and the fixed condition of his eyes which prevented their focusing only at a certain distance, finishing his story—to explain his empty sleeve—with a graphic account of the fight with the bear.

"And I have studied it all out," he said, in conclusion. "I was drugged—I believe, with hasheesh, which makes a man see strange things—and brought up on the bridge lookout where I could be watched and my ravings listened to and recorded, for the sole purpose of discrediting my threatened testimony in regard to the collision of the night before. But I was only half-drugged, as I spilled part of my tea at supper. In that tea, I am positive, was the hasheesh."

"You know all about it, don't you," snarled Captain Bryce, from his chair, "'twas not hasheesh; 'twas an infusion of Indian hemp; you don't know—" Mr. Austen's hand closed over his mouth and he subsided.

"Self-convicted," said Rowland, with a quiet laugh. "Hasheesh is made from Indian hemp."

"You hear this, gentlemen," exclaimed Mr. Meyer, springing to his feet and facing everybody in turn. He pounced on Captain Barry. "You hear this confession, captain; you hear him say Indian hemp? I have a witness now, Mr. Thompson. Go right on with your suit. You hear him, Captain Barry. You are disinterested. You are a witness. You hear?"

"Yes, I heard it—the murdering scoundrel," said the captain.

Mr. Meyer danced up and down in his joy, while the attorney, pocketing his notes, remarked to the discomfited Captain Bryce: "You are the poorest fool I know," and left the office.

Then Mr. Meyer calmed himself, and facing the two steamship officers, said, slowly and impressively, while he poked his forefinger almost into their faces:

"England is a fine country, my friends—a fine country to leave pehind sometimes. Dere is Canada, and der United States, and Australia, and South Africa—all fine countries, too—fine countries to go to with new names. My friends, you will be bulletined and listed at Lloyds in less than half an hour, and you will never again sail under der English flag as officers. And, my friends, let me say, that in half an hour after you are bulletined, all Scotland Yard will be looking for you. But my door is not locked."

Silently they arose, pale, shamefaced, and crushed, and went out the door, through the outer office, and into the street.

CHAPTER XIII

Mr. Selfridge had begun to take an interest in the proceedings. As the two men passed out he arose and asked:

"Have you reached a settlement, Mr. Meyer? Will the insurance be paid?"

"No," roared the underwriter, in the ear of the puzzled old gentleman; while he slapped him vigorously on the back; "it will not be paid. You or I must have been ruined, Mr. Selfridge, and it has settled on you. I do not pay der *Titan's* insurance—nor will der other insurers. On der contrary, as der collision clause in der policy is void with der rest, your company must reimburse me for der insurance which I must pay to der *Royal Age* owners—that is, unless our good friend here, Mr. Rowland, who was on der lookout at der time, will swear that her lights were out."

"Not at all," said Rowland. "Her lights were burning—look to the old gentleman," he exclaimed. "Look out for him. Catch him!"

Mr. Selfridge was stumbling toward a chair. He grasped it, loosened his hold, and before anyone could reach him, fell to the floor, where he lay, with ashen lips and rolling eyes, gasping convulsively.

"Heart failure," said Rowland, as he knelt by his side. "Send for a doctor."

"Send for a doctor," repeated Mr. Meyer through the door to his clerks; "and send for a carriage, quick. I don't want him to die in der office."

Captain Barry lifted the helpless figure to a couch, and they watched, while the convulsions grew easier, the breath shorter, and the lips from ashen gray to blue. Before a doctor or carriage had come, he had passed away.

"Sudden emotion of some kind," said the doctor when he did arrive. "Violent emotion, too. Hear bad news?"

"Bad and good," answered the underwriter. "Good, in learning that this dear little girl was his granddaughter—bad, in learning that he was a ruined man. He was der heaviest stockholder in der *Titan*. One hundred thousand pounds, he owned, of der stock, all of which this poor, dear little child will not get." Mr. Meyer looked sorrowful, as he patted Myra on the head.

Captain Barry beckoned to Rowland, who, slightly flushed, was standing by the still figure on the couch and watching the face of Mr. Meyer, on which annoyance, jubilation, and simulated shock could be seen in turn.

"Wait," he said, as he turned to watch the doctor leave the room. "Is this so, Mr. Meyer," he added to the underwriter, "that Mr. Selfridge owned *Titan* stock, and would have been ruined, had he lived, by the loss of the insurance money?"

"Yes, he would have been a poor man. He had invested his last farthing—one hundred thousand pounds. And if he had left any more it would be assessed to make good his share of what der company must bay for der *Royal Age*, which I also insured."

"Was there a collision clause in the *Titan's* policy?"

"Dere was."

"And you took the risk, knowing that she was to run the Northern Lane at full speed through fog and snow?"

"I did—so did others."

"Then, Mr. Meyer, it remains for me to tell you that the insurance on the *Titan* will be paid, as well as any liabilities included in and specified by the collision clause in the policy. In short, I, the one man who can prevent it, refuse to testify."

"Vwhat-a-t?"

Mr. Meyer grasped the back of a chair and, leaning over it, stared at Rowland.

"You will not testify? Vwhat you mean?"

"What I said; and I do not feel called upon to give you my reasons, Mr. Meyer."

"My good friend," said the underwriter, advancing with outstretched hands to Rowland, who backed away, and taking Myra by the hand, moved toward the door. Mr. Meyer sprang ahead, locked it and removed the key, and faced them.

"Oh, mine goot Gott," he shouted, relapsing in his excitement into the more pronounced dialect of his race; "vwhat I do to you, hey? Vwhy you go pack on me, hey? Haf I not bay der doctor's bill? Haf I not bay for der carriage? Haf I not treat you like one shentleman? Haf I not, hey? I sit you down in mine office and call you Mr. Rowland. Haf I not been one shentleman?"

"Open that door," said Rowland, quietly.

"Yes, open it," repeated Captain Barry, his puzzled face clearing at the prospect of action on his part. "Open it or I'll kick it down."

"But you, mine friend—heard der admission of der captain—of der drugging. One goot witness will do: two is petter. But you will swear, mine friend, you will not ruin me."

"I stand by Rowland," said the captain, grimly. "I don't remember what was said, anyhow; got a blamed bad memory. Get away from that door."

Grievous lamentation—weepings and wailings, and the most genuine gnashing of teeth—interspersed with the feebler cries of the frightened Myra and punctuated by terse commands in regard to the door, filled that private office, to the wonder of the clerks without, and ended, at last, with the crashing of the door from its hinges.

Captain Barry, Rowland, and Myra, followed by a parting, heart-borne malediction from the agitated underwriter, left the office and reached the street. The carriage that had brought them was still waiting.

"Settle inside," called the captain to the driver. "We'll take another, Rowland."

Around the first corner they found a cab, which they entered, Captain Barry giving the driver the direction—"Bark *Peerless*, East India Dock."

"I think I understand the game, Rowland," he said, as they started; "you don't want to break this child."

"That's it," answered Rowland, weakly, as he leaned back on the cushion, faint from the excitement of the last few moments. "And as

for the right or wrong of the position I am in—why, we must go
farther back for it than the question of lookouts. The cause of the
wreck was full speed in a fog. All hands on lookout could not have
seen that berg. The underwriters knew the speed and took the risk.
Let them pay."

"Right—and I'm with you on it. But you must get out of the country. I
don't know the law on the matter, but they may compel you to testify.
You can't ship 'fore the mast again—that's settled. But you can have a
berth mate with me as long as I sail a ship—if you'll take it; and
you're to make my cabin your home as long as you like; remember
that. Still, I know you want to get across with the kid, and if you stay
around until I sail it may be months before you get to New York, with
the chance of losing her by getting foul of English law. But just leave
it to me. There are powerful interests at stake in regard to this
matter."

What Captain Barry had in mind, Rowland was too weak to inquire.
On their arrival at the bark he was assisted by his friend to a couch in
the cabin, where he spent the rest of the day, unable to leave it.
Meanwhile, Captain Barry had gone ashore again.

Returning toward evening, he said to the man on the couch: "I've got
your pay, Rowland, and signed a receipt for it to that attorney. He
paid it out of his own pocket. You could have worked that company
for fifty thousand, or more; but I knew you wouldn't touch their
money, and so, only struck him for your wages. You're entitled to a
month's pay. Here it is—American money—about seventeen." He
gave Rowland a roll of bills.

"Now here's something else, Rowland," he continued, producing an
envelope. "In consideration of the fact that you lost all your clothes
and later, your arm, through the carelessness of the company's
officers, Mr. Thompson offers you this." Rowland opened the
envelope. In it were two first cabin tickets from Liverpool to New
York. Flushing hotly, he said, bitterly:

"It seems that I'm not to escape it, after all."

"Take 'em, old man, take 'em; in fact, I took 'em for you, and you and
the kid are booked. And I made Thompson agree to settle your
doctor's bill and expenses with that Sheeny. 'Tisn't bribery. I'd heel

you myself for the run over, but, hang it, you'll take nothing from me. You've got to get the young un over. You're the only one to do it. The old gentleman was an American, alone here—hadn't even a lawyer, that I could find. The boat sails in the morning and the night train leaves in two hours. Think of that mother, Rowland. Why, man, I'd travel round the world to stand in your shoes when you hand Myra over. I've got a child of my own." The captain's eyes were winking hard and fast, and Rowland's were shining.

"Yes, I'll take the passage," he said, with a smile. "I accept the bribe."

"That's right. You'll be strong and healthy when you land, and when that mother's through thanking you, and you have to think of yourself, remember—I want a mate and will be here a month before sailing. Write to me, care o' Lloyds, if you want the berth, and I'll send you advance money to get back with."

"Thank you, captain," said Rowland, as he took the other's hand and then glanced at his empty sleeve; "but my going to sea is ended. Even a mate needs two hands."

"Well, suit yourself, Rowland; I'll take you mate without any hands at all while you had your brains. It's done me good to meet a man like you; and—say, old man, you won't take it wrong from me, will you? It's none o' my business, but you're too all-fired good a man to drink. You haven't had a nip for two months. Are you going to begin?"

"Never again," said Rowland, rising. "I've a future now, as well as a past."

CHAPTER XIV

It was near noon of the next day that Rowland, seated in a steamer-chair with Myra and looking out on a sail-spangled stretch of blue from the saloon-deck of a west-bound liner, remembered that he had made no provisions to have Mrs. Selfridge notified by cable of the safety of her child; and unless Mr. Meyer or his associates gave the story to the press it would not be known.

"Well," he mused, "joy will not kill, and I shall witness it in its fullness if I take her by surprise. But the chances are that it will get into the papers before I reach her. It is too good for Mr. Meyer to keep."

But the story was not given out immediately. Mr. Meyer called a conference of the underwriters concerned with him in the insurance of the *Titan* at which it was decided to remain silent concerning the card they hoped to play, and to spend a little time and money in hunting for other witnesses among the *Titan's* crew, and in interviewing Captain Barry, to the end of improving his memory. A few stormy meetings with this huge obstructionist convinced them of the futility of further effort in his direction, and, after finding at the end of a week that every surviving member of the *Titan's* port watch, as well as a few of the other, had been induced to sign for Cape voyages, or had otherwise disappeared, they decided to give the story told by Rowland to the press in the hope that publicity would avail to bring to light corroboratory evidence.

And this story, improved upon in the repeating by Mr. Meyer to reporters, and embellished still further by the reporters as they wrote it up, particularly in the part pertaining to the polar bear,—blazoned out in the great dailies of England and the Continent, and was cabled to New York, with the name of the steamer in which John Rowland had sailed (for his movements had been traced in the search for evidence), where it arrived, too late for publication, the morning of the day on which, with Myra on his shoulder, he stepped down the gang-plank at a North River dock. As a consequence, he was surrounded on the dock by enthusiastic reporters, who spoke of the story and asked for details. He refused to talk, escaped them, and gaining the side streets, soon found himself in crowded Broadway, where he entered the office of the steamship company in whose employ he had been wrecked, and secured from the *Titan's* passenger-list the address of Mrs. Selfridge—the only woman saved. Then he took a car up Broadway and alighted abreast of a large department store.

"We're going to see mamma, soon, Myra," he whispered in the pink ear; "and you must go dressed up. It don't matter about me; but you're a Fifth Avenue baby—a little aristocrat. These old clothes won't do, now." But she had forgotten the word "mamma," and was more interested in the exciting noise and life of the street than in the clothing she wore. In the store, Rowland asked for, and was directed to the children's department, where a young woman waited on him.

"This child has been shipwrecked," he said. "I have sixteen dollars and a half to spend on it. Give it a bath, dress its hair, and use up the money on a dress, shoes, and stockings, underclothing, and a hat." The young woman stooped and kissed the little girl from sheer sympathy, but protested that not much could be done.

"Do your best," said Rowland; "it is all I have. I will wait here."

An hour later, penniless again, he emerged from the store with Myra, bravely dressed in her new finery, and was stopped at the corner by a policeman who had seen him come out, and who marveled, doubtless, at such juxtaposition of rags and ribbons.

"Whose kid ye got?" he demanded.

"I believe it is the daughter of Mrs. Colonel Selfridge," answered Rowland, haughtily—too haughtily, by far.

"Ye believe—but ye don't know. Come back into the shtore, me tourist, and we'll see who ye shtole it from."

"Very well, officer; I can prove possession." They started back, the officer with his hand on Rowland's collar, and were met at the door by a party of three or four people coming out. One of this party, a young woman in black, uttered a piercing shriek and sprang toward them.

"Myra!" she screamed. "Give me my baby—give her to me."

She snatched the child from Rowland's shoulder, hugged it, kissed it, cried, and screamed over it; then, oblivious to the crowd that collected, incontinently fainted in the arms of an indignant old gentleman.

"You scoundrel!" he exclaimed, as he flourished his cane over Rowland's head with his free arm. "We've caught you. Officer, take that man to the station-house. I will follow and make a charge in the name of my daughter."

"Then he shtole the kid, did he?" asked the policeman.

"Most certainly," answered the old gentleman, as, with the assistance of the others, he supported the unconscious young mother to a carriage. They all entered, little Myra screaming for Rowland from the arms of a female member of the party, and were driven off.

"C'm an wi' me," uttered the officer, rapping his prisoner on the head with his club and jerking him off his feet.

Then, while an approving crowd applauded, the man who had fought and conquered a hungry polar bear was dragged through the streets like a sick animal by a New York policeman. For such is the stultifying effect of a civilized environment.

CHAPTER XV

In New York City there are homes permeated by a moral atmosphere so pure, so elevated, so sensitive to the vibrations of human woe and misdoing, that their occupants are removed completely from all consideration of any but the spiritual welfare of poor humanity. In these homes the news-gathering, sensation-mongering daily paper does not enter.

In the same city are dignified magistrates—members of clubs and societies—who spend late hours, and often fail to arise in the morning in time to read the papers before the opening of court.

Also in New York are city editors, bilious of stomach, testy of speech, and inconsiderate of reporters' feelings and professional pride. Such editors, when a reporter has failed, through no fault of his own, in successfully interviewing a celebrity, will sometimes send him news-gathering in the police courts, where printable news is scarce.

On the morning following the arrest of John Rowland, three reporters, sent by three such editors, attended a hall of justice presided over by one of the late-rising magistrates mentioned above. In the anteroom of this court, ragged, disfigured by his clubbing, and disheveled by his night in a cell, stood Rowland, with other unfortunates more or less guilty of offense against society. When his name was called, he was hustled through a door, along a line of policemen—each of whom added to his own usefulness by giving him a shove—and into the dock, where the stern-faced and tired-looking magistrate glared at him. Seated in a corner of the court-room were the old gentleman of the day before, the young mother with little Myra in her lap, and a number of other ladies—all excited in demeanor; and all but the young mother directing venomous glances at Rowland. Mrs. Selfridge, pale and hollow-eyed, but happy-faced, withal, allowed no wandering glance to rest on him.

The officer who had arrested Rowland was sworn, and testified that he had stopped the prisoner on Broadway while making off with the child, whose rich clothing had attracted his attention. Disdainful sniffs were heard in the corner with muttered remarks: "Rich indeed—the idea—the flimsiest prints." Mr. Gaunt, the prosecuting witness, was called to testify.

"This man, your Honor," he began, excitedly, "was once a gentleman and a frequent guest at my house. He asked for the hand of my daughter, and as his request was not granted, threatened revenge. Yes, sir. And out on the broad Atlantic, where he had followed my daughter in the guise of a sailor, he attempted to murder that child—my grandchild; but was discovered—"

"Wait," interrupted the magistrate. "Confine your testimony to the present offense."

"Yes, your Honor. Failing in this, he stole, or enticed the little one from its bed, and in less than five minutes the ship was wrecked, and he must have escaped with the child in—"

"Were you a witness of this?"

"I was not there, your Honor; but we have it on the word of the first officer, a gentleman—"

"Step down, sir. That will do. Officer, was this offense committed in New York?"

"Yes, your Honor; I caught him meself."

"Who did he steal the child from?"

"That leddy over yonder."

"Madam, will you take the stand?"

With her child in her arms, Mrs. Selfridge was sworn and in a low, quavering voice repeated what her father had said. Being a woman, she was allowed by the woman-wise magistrate to tell her story in her own way. When she spoke of the attempted murder at the taffrail, her manner became excited. Then she told of the captain's promise to put the man in irons on her agreeing to testify against him—of the consequent decrease in her watchfulness, and her missing the child just before the shipwreck—of her rescue by the gallant first officer, and his assertion that he had seen her child in the arms of this man—the only man on earth who would harm it—of the later news that a boat containing sailors and children had been picked up by a Mediterranean steamer—of the detectives sent over, and their report that a sailor answering this man's description had refused to surrender a child to the consul at Gibraltar and had disappeared with it—of her joy at the news that Myra was alive, and despair of ever seeing her again until she had met her in this man's arms on Broadway the day before. At this point, outraged maternity overcame her. With cheeks flushed, and eyes blazing scorn and anger, she pointed at Rowland and all but screamed: "And he has mutilated—tortured my baby. There are deep wounds in her little back, and the doctor said, only last night, that they were made by a sharp instrument. And he must have tried to warp and twist the mind of my child, or put her through frightful experiences; for he has taught her to swear—horribly—and last night at bedtime, when I told her the story of Elisha and the bears and the children, she burst out into the most uncontrollable screaming and sobbing."

Here her testimony ended in a breakdown of hysterics, between sobs of which were frequent admonitions to the child not to say that bad word; for Myra had caught sight of Rowland and was calling his nickname.

"What shipwreck was this—where was it?" asked the puzzled magistrate of nobody in particular.

"The *Titan*," called out half a dozen newspaper men across the room.

"The *Titan*," repeated the magistrate. "Then this offense was committed on the high seas under the English flag. I cannot imagine why it is brought into this court. Prisoner, have you anything to say?"

"Nothing, your Honor." The answer came in a kind of dry sob.

The magistrate scanned the ashen-faced man in rags, and said to the clerk of the court: "Change this charge to vagrancy—eh—"

The clerk, instigated by the newspaper men, was at his elbow. He laid a morning paper before him, pointed to certain big letters and retired. Then the business of the court suspended while the court read the news. After a moment or two the magistrate looked up.

"Prisoner," he said, sharply, "take your left sleeve out of your breast!" Rowland obeyed mechanically, and it dangled at his side. The magistrate noticed, and read on. Then he folded the paper and said:

"You are the man who was rescued from an iceberg, are you not?" The prisoner bowed his head.

"Discharged!" The word came forth in an unjudicial roar. "Madam," added the magistrate, with a kindling light in his eye, "this man has merely saved your child's life. If you will read of his defending it from a polar bear when you go home, I doubt that you will tell it any more bear stories. Sharp instrument—umph!" Which was equally unjudicial on the part of the court.

Mrs. Selfridge, with a mystified and rather aggrieved expression of face, left the court-room with her indignant father and friends, while Myra shouted profanely for Rowland, who had fallen into the hands of the reporters. They would have entertained him after the manner of the craft, but he would not be entertained—neither would he talk. He escaped and was swallowed up in the world without; and when the evening papers appeared that day, the events of the trial were all that could be added to the story of the morning.

CHAPTER XVI

On the morning of the next day, a one-armed dock lounger found an old fish-hook and some pieces of string which he knotted together; then he dug some bait and caught a fish. Being hungry and without fire, he traded with a coaster's cook for a meal, and before night caught two more, one of which he traded, the other, sold. He slept under the docks—paying no rent—fished, traded, and sold for a month, then paid for a second-hand suit of clothes and the services of a barber. His changed appearance induced a boss stevedore to hire him tallying cargo, which was more lucrative than fishing, and furnished, in time, a hat, pair of shoes, and an overcoat. He then rented a room and slept in a bed. Before long he found employment addressing envelopes for a mailing firm, at which his fine and rapid penmanship secured him steady work; and in a few months he asked his employers to indorse his application for a Civil Service examination. The favor was granted, the examination easily passed, and he addressed envelopes while he waited. Meanwhile he bought new and better clothing and seemed to have no difficulty in impressing those whom he met with the fact that he was a gentleman. Two years from the time of his examination he was appointed to a lucrative position under the Government, and as he seated himself at the desk in his office, could have been heard to remark: "Now John Rowland, your future is your own. You have merely suffered in the past from a mistaken estimate of the importance of women and whisky."

But he was wrong, for in six months he received a letter which, in part, read as follows:

"Do not think me indifferent or ungrateful. I have watched from a distance while you made your wonderful fight for your old standards. You have won, and I am glad and I congratulate you. But Myra will not let me rest. She asks for you continually and cries at times. I can bear it no longer. Will you not come and see Myra?"

And the man went to see—Myra.

BEYOND THE SPECTRUM

The long-expected crisis was at hand, and the country was on the verge of war. Jingoism was rampant. Japanese laborers were mobbed on the western slope, Japanese students were hazed out of colleges, and Japanese children stoned away from playgrounds. Editorial pages sizzled with burning words of patriotism; pulpits thundered with invocations to the God of battles and prayers for the perishing of the way of the ungodly. Schoolboy companies were formed and paraded with wooden guns; amateur drum-corps beat time to the throbbing of the public pulse; militia regiments, battalions, and separate companies of infantry and artillery, drilled, practiced, and paraded; while the regular army was rushed to the posts and garrisons of the Pacific Coast, and the navy, in three divisions, guarded the Hawaiian Islands, the Philippines, and the larger ports of western America. For Japan had a million trained men, with transports to carry them, battle-ships to guard them; with the choice of objective when she was ready to strike; and she was displaying a national secrecy about her choice especially irritating to molders of public opinion and lovers of fair play. War was not yet declared by either side, though the Japanese minister at Washington had quietly sailed for Europe on private business, and the American minister at Tokio, with several consuls and clerks scattered around the ports of Japan, had left their jobs hurriedly, for reasons connected with their general health. This was the situation when the cabled news from Manila told of the staggering into port of the scout cruiser *Salem* with a steward in command, a stoker at the wheel, the engines in charge of firemen, and the captain, watch-officers, engineers, seamen gunners, and the whole fighting force of the ship stricken with a form of partial blindness which in some cases promised to become total.

The cruiser was temporarily out of commission and her stricken men in the hospital; but by the time the specialists had diagnosed the trouble as amblyopia, from some sudden shock to the optic nerve—followed in cases by complete atrophy, resulting in amaurosis—another ship came into Honolulu in the same predicament. Like the other craft four thousand miles away, her deck force had been stricken suddenly and at night. Still another, a battle-ship, followed into Honolulu, with fully five hundred more or less blind men groping around her decks; and the admiral on the station called in all the outriders by wireless. They came as they could, some hitting sand-bars or shoals on the way, and every one crippled and helpless to fight. The diagnosis was the same—amblyopia, atrophy of the nerve, and incipient amaurosis; which in plain language meant dimness of vision increasing to blindness.

Then came more news from Manila. Ship after ship came in, or was towed in, with fighting force sightless, and the work being done by the "black gang" or the idlers, and each with the same report—the gradual dimming of lights and outlines as the night went on, resulting in partial or total blindness by sunrise. And now it was remarked that those who escaped were the lower-deck workers, those whose duties kept them off the upper deck and away from gunports and deadlights. It was also suggested that the cause was some deadly attribute of the night air in these tropical regions, to which the Americans succumbed; for, so far, the coast division had escaped.

In spite of the efforts of the Government, the Associated Press got the facts, and the newspapers of the country changed the burden of their pronouncements. Bombastic utterances gave way to bitter criticism of an inefficient naval policy that left the ships short of fighters in a crisis. The merging of the line and the staff, which had excited much ridicule when inaugurated, now received more intelligent attention. Former critics of the change not only condoned it, but even demanded the wholesale granting of commissions to skippers and mates of the merchant service; and insisted that surgeons, engineers, paymasters, and chaplains, provided they could still see to box the compass, should be given command of the torpedo craft and smaller scouts. All of which made young Surgeon Metcalf, on waiting orders at San Francisco, smile sweetly and darkly to himself: for his last appointment had been the command of a hospital ship, in which position, though a seaman, navigator, and graduate of Annapolis, he had been made the subject of newspaper ridicule and official controversy, and had even been caricatured as going into battle in a ship armored with court-plaster and armed with hypodermic syringes.

Metcalf had resigned as ensign to take up the study and practice of medicine, but at the beginning of the war scare had returned to his first love, relinquishing a lucrative practice as eye-specialist to tender his services to the Government. And the Government had responded by ranking him with his class as junior lieutenant, and giving him the aforesaid command, which he was glad to be released from. But his classmates and brother officers had not responded so promptly with their welcome, and Metcalf found himself combating a naval etiquette that was nearly as intolerant of him as of other appointees from civil life. It embittered him a little, but he pulled through; for he was a likable young fellow, with a cheery face and pleasant voice, and even the most hide-bound product of Annapolis could not long resist his personality. So he was not entirely barred out of official gossip and speculations, and soon had an opportunity to question some convalescents sent home from Honolulu. All told the same story and described the same symptoms, but one added an extra one. An itching and burning of the face had accompanied the attack, such as is produced by sunburn.

"And where were you that night when it came?" asked Metcalf, eagerly.

"On the bridge with the captain and watch-officers. It was all hands that night. We had made out a curious light to the north'ard, and were trying to find out what it was."

"What kind of a light?"

"Well, it was rather faint, and seemed to be about a mile away. Sometimes it looked red, then green, or yellow, or blue."

"And then it disappeared?"

"Yes, and though we steamed toward it with all the searchlights at work, we never found where it came from."

"What form did it take—a beam or a glow?"

"It wasn't a glow—radiation—and it didn't seem to be a beam. It was an occasional flash, and in this sense was like a radiation—that is, like the spokes of a wheel, each spoke with its own color. But that was at the beginning. In three hours none of us could have distinguished colors."

Metcalf soon had an opportunity to question others. The first batch of invalid officers arrived from Manila, and these, on being pressed, admitted that they had seen colored lights at the beginning of the night. These, Metcalf remarked, were watch-officers, whose business was to look for strange lights and investigate them. But one of them added this factor to the problem.

"And it was curious about Brainard, the most useless and utterly incompetent man ever graduated. He was so near-sighted that he couldn't see the end of his nose without glasses; but it was he that took the ship in, with the rest of us eating with our fingers and asking our way to the sick-bay."

"And Brainard wore his glasses that night?'" asked Metcalf.

"Yes; he couldn't see without them. It reminds me of Nydia, the blind girl who piloted a bunch out of Pompeii because she was used to the darkness. Still, Brainard is hardly a parallel."

"Were his glasses the ordinary kind, or pebbles?"

"Don't know. Which are the cheapest? That's the kind."

"The ordinary kind."

"Well, he had the ordinary kind—like himself. And he'll get special promotion. Oh, Lord! He'll be jumped up a dozen numbers."

"Well," said Metcalf, mysteriously, "perhaps not. Just wait."

Metcalf kept his counsel, and in two weeks there came Japan's declaration of war in a short curt note to the Powers at Washington. Next day the papers burned with news, cabled *via* St. Petersburg and London, of the sailing of the Japanese fleet from its home station, but for where was not given—in all probability either the Philippines or the Hawaiian Islands. But when, next day, a torpedo-boat came into San Francisco in command of the cook, with his mess-boy at the wheel, conservatism went to the dogs, and bounties were offered for enlistment at the various navy-yards, while commissions were made out as fast as they could be signed, and given to any applicant who could even pretend to a knowledge of yachts. And Surgeon George Metcalf, with the rank of junior lieutenant, was ordered to the torpedo-boat above mentioned, and with him as executive officer a young graduate of the academy, Ensign Smith, who with the enthusiasm and courage of youth combined the mediocrity of inexperience and the full share of the service prejudice against civilians.

This prejudice remained in full force, unmodified by the desperate situation of the country; and the unstricken young officers filling subordinate positions on the big craft, while congratulating him, openly denied his moral right to a command that others had earned a better right to by remaining in the service; and the old jokes, jibes, and satirical references to syringes and sticking-plaster whirled about his head as he went to and fro, fitting out his boat and laying in supplies. And when they learned—from young Mr. Smith—that among these supplies was a large assortment of plain-glass spectacles, of no magnifying power whatever, the ridicule was unanimous and heartfelt; even the newspapers taking up the case from the old standpoint and admitting that the line ought to be drawn at lunatics and foolish people. But Lieutenant Metcalf smiled and went quietly ahead, asking for and receiving orders to scout.

He received them the more readily, as all the scouts in the squadron, including the torpedo-flotilla and two battle-ships, had come in with blinded crews. Their stories were the same—they had all seen the mysterious colored lights, had gone blind, and a few had felt the itching and tingling of sunburn. And the admiral gleaned one crew of whole men from the fleet, and with it manned his best ship, the *Delaware.*

Metcalf went to sea, and was no sooner outside the Golden Gate than he opened his case of spectacles, and scandalized all hands, even his executive officer, by stern and explicit orders to wear them night and day, putting on a pair himself as an example.

A few of the men attested good eyesight; but this made no difference, he explained. They were to wear them or take the consequences, and as the first man to take the consequences was Mr. Smith, whom he sent to his room for twenty-four hours for appearing on deck without them five minutes afterward, the men concluded that he was in earnest and obeyed the order, though with smiles and silent ridicule. Another explicit command they received more readily: to watch out for curious-looking craft, and for small objects such as floating casks, capsized tubs or boats, et cetera. And this brought results the day after the penitent Smith was released. They sighted a craft without spars steaming along on the horizon and ran down to her. She was a sealer, the skipper explained, when hailed, homeward bound under the auxiliary. She had been on fire, but the cause of the fire was a mystery. A few days before a strange-looking vessel had passed them, a mile away. She was a whaleback sort of a hull, with sloping ends, without spars or funnels, only a slim pole amidships, and near its base a projection that looked like a liner's crow's-nest. While they watched, their foremast burst into flames, and while they were rigging their hose the mainmast caught fire. Before this latter was well under way they noticed a round hole burnt deeply into the mast, of about four inches diameter. Next, the topsides caught fire, and they had barely saved their craft, letting their masts burn to do so.

"Was it a bright, sunshiny day?" asked Metcalf.

"Sure. Four days ago. He was heading about sou'west, and going slow."

"Anything happen to your eyesight?"

"Say—yes. One of my men's gone stone blind. Thinks he must have looked squarely at the sun when he thought he was looking at the fire up aloft."

"It wasn't the sun. Keep him in utter darkness for a week at least. He'll get well. What was your position when you met that fellow?"

"About six hundred miles due nor'west from here."

"All right. Look out for Japanese craft. War is declared."

Metcalf plotted a new course, designed to intercept that of the mysterious craft, and went on, so elated by the news he had heard that he took his gossipy young executive into his confidence.

"Mr. Smith," he said, "that sealer described one of the new seagoing submersibles of the Japanese, did he not?"

"Yes, sir, I think he did—a larger submarine, without any conning-tower and the old-fashioned periscope. They have seven thousand miles' cruising radius, enough to cross the Pacific."

By asking questions of various craft, and by diligent use of a telescope, Metcalf found his quarry three days later—a log-like object on the horizon, with the slim white pole amidships and the excrescence near its base.

"Wait till I get his bearing by compass," said Metcalf to his chief officer, "then we'll smoke up our specs and run down on him. Signal him by the International Code to put out his light, and to heave to, or we'll sink him."

Mr. Smith bowed to his superior, found the numbers of these commands in the code book, and with a string of small flags at the signal-yard, and every man aboard viewing the world darkly through a smoky film, the torpedo-boat approached the stranger at thirty knots. But there was no blinding glare of light in their eyes, and when they were within a hundred yards of the submersible, Metcalf removed his glasses for a moment's distinct vision. Head and shoulders out of a hatch near the tube was a man waving a white handkerchief. He rang the stopping bells.

"He surrenders, Mr. Smith," he said, joyously, "and without firing a torpedo!"

He examined the man through the telescope and laughed.

"I know him," he said. Then funneling his hands, he hailed:

"Do you surrender to the United States of America?"

"I surrender," answered the man. "I am helpless."

"Then come aboard without arms. I'll send a boat."

A small dinghy-like boat was dispatched, and it returned with the man, a Japanese in lieutenant's uniform, whose beady eyes twinkled in alarm as Metcalf greeted him.

"Well, Saiksi, you perfected it, didn't you?—my invisible searchlight, that I hadn't money to go on with."

The Jap's eyes sought the deck, then resumed their Asiatic steadiness.

"Metcalf—this you," he said, "in command? I investigated and heard you had resigned to become a doctor."

"But I came back to the service, Saiksi. Thanks to you and your light—my light, rather—I am in command here in place of men you blinded. Saiksi, you deserve no consideration from me, in spite of our rooming together at Annapolis. You took—I don't say stole my invention, and turned it against the country that educated you. You, or your *confrères*, did this before a declaration of war. You are a pirate, and I could string you up to my signal-yard and escape criticism."

"I was under orders from my superiors, Captain Metcalf."

"They shall answer to mine. You shall answer to me. How many boats have you equipped with my light?"

"There are but three. It is very expensive."

"One for our Philippine squadron, one for the Hawaiian, and one for the coast. You overdid things, Saiksi. If you hadn't set fire to that sealer the other day, I might not have found you. It was a senseless piece of work that did you no good. Oh, you are a sweet character! How do you get your ultraviolet rays—by filtration or prismatic dispersion?"

"By filtration."

"Saiksi, you're a liar as well as a thief. The colored lights you use to attract attention are the discarded rays of the spectrum. No wonder you investigated me before you dared flash such a decoy! Well, I'm back in the navy, and I've been investigating you. As soon as I heard of the first symptom of sunburn, I knew it was caused by the ultraviolet rays, the same as from the sun; and I knew that nothing but my light could produce those rays at night time. And as a physician I knew what I did not know as an inventor—the swift amblyopia that follows the impact of this light on the retina. As a physician, too, I can inform you that your country has not permanently blinded a single American seaman or officer. The effects wear off."

The Jap gazed stolidly before him while Metcalf delivered himself of this, but did not reply.

"Where is the Japanese fleet bound?" he asked, sternly.

"I do not know."

"And would not tell, whether you knew or not. But you said you were helpless. What has happened to you? You can tell that."

"A simple thing, Captain Metcalf. My supply of oil leaked away, and my engines must work slowly. Your signal was useless; I could not have turned on the light."

"You have answered the first question. You are far from home without a mother-ship, or she would have found you and furnished oil before this. You have come thus far expecting the fleet to follow and strike a helpless coast before your supplies ran out."

Again the Jap's eyes dropped in confusion, and Metcalf went on.

"I can refurnish your boat with oil, my engineer and my men can handle her, and I can easily learn to manipulate your—or shall I say *our*—invisible searchlight. Hail your craft in English and order all hands on deck unarmed, ready for transshipment to this boat. I shall join your fleet myself."

A man was lounging in the hatchway of the submersible, and this man Saiksi hailed.

"Ae-hai, ae-hai, Matsu. We surrender. We are prisoner. Call up all men onto the deck. Leave arms behind. We are prisoner."

They mustered eighteen in all, and in half an hour they were ironed in a row along the stanchioned rail of the torpedo-boat.

"You, too, Saiksi," said Metcalf, coming toward him with a pair of jingling handcuffs.

"Is it not customary, Captain Metcalf," said the Jap, "to parole a surrendered commander?"

"Not the surrendered commander of a craft that uses new and deadly weapons of war unknown to her adversary, and before the declaration of war. Hold up your hands. You're going into irons with your men. All Japs look alike to me, now."

So Lieutenant Saiksi, of the Japanese navy, was ironed beside his cook and meekly sat down on the deck. With the difference of dress, they really did look alike.

Metcalf had thirty men in his crew. With the assistance of his engineer, a man of mechanics, he picked eighteen of this crew and took them and a barrel of oil aboard the submersible. Then for three days the two craft lay together, while the engineer and the men familiarized themselves with her internal economy—the torpedo-tubes, gasoline engines, storage-batteries, and motors; and the vast system of pipes, valves, and wires that gave life and action to the boat—and while Metcalf experimented with the mysterious searchlight attached to the periscope tube invented by himself, but perfected by others. Part of his investigation extended into the night. Externally, the light resembled a huge cup about two feet in diameter, with a thick disk fitted around it in a vertical plane. This disk he removed; then, hailing Smith to rig his fire-hose and get off the deck, he descended the hatchway and turned on the light, viewing its effects through the periscope. This, be it known, is merely a perpendicular, non-magnifying telescope that, by means of a reflector at its upper end, gives a view of the seascape when a submarine boat is submerged. And in the eyepiece at its base Metcalf beheld a thin thread of light, of such dazzling brilliancy as to momentarily blind him, stretch over the sea; but he put on his smoked glasses and turned the apparatus, tube and all, until the thin pencil of light touched the end of the torpedo-boat's signal-yard. He did not need to bring the two-inch beam to a focus; it burst into flame and he quickly shut off the light and shouted to Smith to put out the fire—which Smith promptly did, with open comment to his handful of men on this destruction of Government property.

"Good enough!" he said to Smith, when next they met. "Now if I'm any good I'll give the Japs a taste of their own medicine."

"Take me along, captain," burst out Smith in sudden surrender. "I don't understand all this, but I want to be in it."

"No, Mr. Smith. The chief might do your work, but I doubt that you could do his. I need him; so you can take the prisoners home. You will undoubtedly retain command."

"Very good, sir," answered the disappointed youngster, trying to conceal his chagrin.

"I don't want you to feel badly about it. I know how you all felt toward me. But I'm on a roving commission. I have no wireless apparatus and no definite instructions. I've been lampooned and ridiculed in the papers, and I'm going to give them my answer—that is, as I said, if I'm any good. If I'm not I'll be sunk."

So when the engineer had announced his mastery of his part of the problem, and that there was enough of gasoline to cruise for two weeks longer, Smith departed with the torpedo-boat, and Metcalf began his search for the expected fleet.

It was more by good luck than by any possible calculation that Metcalf finally found the fleet. A steamer out of San Francisco reported that it had not been heard from, and one bound in from Honolulu said that it was not far behind—in fact had sent a shot or two. Metcalf shut off gasoline, waited a day, and saw the smoke on the horizon. Then he submerged to the awash condition, which in this boat just floated the searchlight out of water; and thus balanced, neither floating nor sinking nor rolling, but rising and falling with the long pulsing of the ground-swell, he watched through the periscope the approach of the enemy.

It was an impressive spectacle, and to a citizen of a threatened country a disquieting one. Nine high-sided battle-ships of ten-gun type—nine floating forts, each one, unopposed, able to reduce to smoking ruin a city out of sight of its gunners; each one impregnable to the shell fire of any fortification in the world, and to the impact of the heaviest torpedo yet constructed—they came silently along in line-ahead formation, like Indians on a trail. There were no compromises in this fleet. Like the intermediate batteries of the ships themselves, cruisers had been eliminated and it consisted of extremes, battle-ships, and torpedo-boats, the latter far to the rear. But between the two were half a dozen colliers, repair, and supply ships.

Night came down before they were near enough for operations, and Metcalf turned on his invisible light, expanding the beam to embrace the fleet in its light, and moved the boat to a position about a mile away from its path. It was a weird picture now showing in the periscope: each gray ship a bluish-green against a background of black marked here and there by the green crest of a breaking sea. Within Metcalf's reach were the levers, cranks, and worms that governed the action of the periscope and the light; just before him were the vertical and horizontal steering-wheels; under these a self-illuminating compass, and at his ear a system of push-buttons, speaking-tubes, and telegraph-dials that put him in communication with every man on the boat, each one of whom had his part to play at the proper moment, but not one of whom could see or know the result. The work to be done was in Metcalf's hands and brain, and, considering its potentiality, it was a most undramatic performance.

He waited until the leading flag-ship was within half a mile of being abreast; then, turning on a hanging electric bulb, he held it close to the eyepiece of the periscope, knowing that the light would go up the tube through the lenses and be visible to the fleet. And in a moment he heard faintly through the steel walls the sound transmitted by the sea of a bugle-call to quarters. He shut off the bulb, watched a wandering shaft of light from the flag-ship seeking him, then contracted his own invisible beam to a diameter of about three feet, to fall upon the flag-ship, and played it back and forth, seeking gun ports and apertures and groups of men, painting all with that blinding light that they could not see, nor immediately sense. There was nothing to indicate that he had succeeded; the faces of the different groups were still turned his way, and the futile searchlight still wandered around, unable to bring to their view the white tube with its cup-like base.

Still waving the wandering beam of white light, the flag-ship passed on, bringing along the second in line, and again Metcalf turned on his bulb. He heard her bugle-call, and saw, in varied shades of green, the twinkling red and blue lights of her masthead signals, received from the flag-ship and passed down the line. And again he played that green disk of deadly light upon the faces of her crew. This ship, too, was seeking him with her searchlight, and soon, from the whole nine, a moving network of brilliant beams flashed and scintillated across the sky; but not one settled upon the cause of their disquiet.

Ship after ship passed on, each with its bugle-call to quarters, each with its muster of all hands to meet the unknown emergency—the menace on a hostile coast of a faint white light on the port beam—but not one firing a shot or shell; there was nothing to fire at. And with the passing of the last of the nine Metcalf listened to a snapping and a buzzing overhead that told of the burning out of the carbons in the light.

"Good work for the expenditure," he murmured, wearily. "Let's see—two carbons and about twenty amperes of current, against nine ships at ten millions apiece. Well, we'll soon know whether or not it worked."

While an electrician rigged new carbons he rested his eyes and his brain; for the mental and physical strain had been severe. Then he played the light upon the colliers and supply ships as they charged by, disposing of them in the same manner, and looked for other craft of larger menace. But there were none, except the torpedo contingent, and these he decided to leave alone. There were fifteen of them, each as speedy and as easily handled as his own craft; and already, apprised by the signaled instructions from ahead, they were spreading out into a fan-like formation, and coming on, nearly abreast.

"The jig's up, chief," he called through a tube to the engineer. "We'll get forty feet down until the mosquitoes get by. I'd like to take a chance at them but there are too many. We'd get torpedoed, surely."

Down went the diving rudder, and, with a kick ahead of the engine, the submersible shot under, heading on a course across the path of the fleet, and in half an hour came to the surface. There was nothing in sight, close by, either through the periscope or by direct vision, and Metcalf decided to make for San Francisco and report.

It was a wise decision, for at daylight he was floundering in a heavy sea and a howling gale from the northwest that soon forced him to submerge again for comfort. Before doing so, however, he enjoyed one good look at the Japanese fleet, far ahead and to port. The line of formation was broken, staggered, and disordered; and, though the big ships were making good weather of it, they were steering badly, and on one of them, half-way to the signal-yard, was the appeal for help that ships of all nations use and recognize—the ensign, upside-down. Under the lee of each ship was snuggled a torpedo-boat, plunging, rolling, and swamped by the breaking seas that even the mighty bulk to windward could not protect them from. And even as Metcalf looked, one twisted in two, her after funnels pointing to port, her forward to starboard, and in ten seconds had disappeared.

Metcalf submerged and went on at lesser speed, but in comfort and safety. Through the periscope he saw one after the other of the torpedo-craft give up the fight they were not designed for, and ship after ship hoist that silent prayer for help. They yawed badly, but in some manner or other managed to follow the flag-ship, which, alone of that armada, steered fairly well. She kept on the course for the Golden Gate.

Even submerged Metcalf outran the fleet before noon, and at night had dropped it, entering the Golden Gate before daylight, still submerged, not only on account of the troublesome turmoil on the surface, but to avoid the equally troublesome scrutiny of the forts, whose searchlights might have caught him had he presented more to their view than a slim tube painted white. Avoiding the mines, he picked his way carefully up to the man-of-war anchorage, and arose to the surface, alongside the *Delaware*, now the flag-ship, as the light of day crept upward in the eastern sky.

"We knew they were on the coast," said the admiral, a little later, when Metcalf had made his report on the quarter-deck of the *Delaware*. "But about this light? Are you sure of all this? Why, if it's so, the President will rank you over us all. Mr. Smith came in with the prisoners, but he said nothing of an invisible light—only of a strong searchlight with which you set fire to the signal-yard."

"I did not tell him all, admiral," answered Metcalf, a little hurt at the persistence of the feeling. "But I'm satisfied now. That fleet is coming on with incompetents on the bridge."

"Well, we'll soon know. I've only one ship, but it's my business to get out and defend the United States against invaders, and as soon as I can steam against this gale and sea I'll go. And I'll want you, too. I'm short-handed."

"Thank you, sir. I shall be glad to be with you. But wouldn't you like to examine the light?"

"Most certainly," said the admiral; and, accompanied by his staff, he followed Metcalf aboard the submersible.

"It is very simple," explained Metcalf, showing a rough diagram he had sketched. "You see he has used my system of reflectors about as I designed it. The focus of one curve coincides with the focus of the next, and the result is a thin beam containing nearly all the radiations of the arc."

"Very simple," remarked the admiral, dryly. "Very simple indeed. But, admitting this strong beam of light that, as you say, could set fire to that sealer, and be invisible in sunshine, how about the beam that is invisible by night? That is what I am wondering about."

"Here, sir," removing the thick disk from around the light. "This contains the prisms, which refract the beam entirely around the lamp; and disperse it into the seven colors of the spectrum. All the visible light is cut out, leaving only the ultraviolet rays, and these travel as fast and as far, and return by reflection, as though accompanied by the visible rays."

"But how can you see it?" asked an officer. "How is the ship it is directed at made visible?"

"By fluorescence," answered Metcalf. "The observer is the periscope itself. Any of the various fluorescing substances placed in the focus of the object-glass, or at the optical image in front of the eyepiece, will show the picture in the color peculiar to the fluorescing material. The color does not matter."

"More simple still," laughed the admiral. "But how about the colored lights they saw?"

"Simply the discarded light of the spectrum. By removing this cover on the disk, the different colored rays shoot up. That was to attract attention. I used only white light through the periscope."

"And it was this invisible light that blinded so many men, which in your hands blinded the crews of the Japanese?" asked the admiral.

"Yes, sir. The ultraviolet rays are beneficial as a germicide, but are deadly if too strong."

"Lieutenant Metcalf," said the admiral, seriously, "your future in the service is secure. I apologize for laughing at you; but now that it's over and you've won, tell us about the spectacles."

"Why, admiral," responded Metcalf, "that was the simplest proposition of all. The whole apparatus—prisms, periscope, lenses, and the fluorescing screen—are made of rock crystal, which is permeable to the ultraviolet light. But common glass, of which spectacles are made, is opaque to it. That is why near-sighted men escaped the blindness."

"Then, unless the Japs are near-sighted, I expect an easy time when I go out."

But the admiral did not need to go out and fight. Those nine big battle-ships that Japan had struggled for years to obtain, and the auxiliary fleet of supply and repair ships to keep them in life and health away from home, caught on a lee shore in a hurricane against which the mighty *Delaware* could not steam to sea, piled up one by one on the sands below Fort Point; and, each with a white flag replacing the reversed ensign, surrendered to the transport or collier sent out to take off the survivors.

IN THE VALLEY OF THE SHADOW

There are few facilities for cooking aboard submarine torpedo-boats, and that is why Lieutenant Ross ran his little submarine up alongside the flag-ship at noon, and made fast to the boat-boom—the horizontal spar extending from warships, to which the boats ride when in the water. And, as familiarity breeds contempt, after the first, tentative, trial, he had been content to let her hang by one of the small, fixed painters depending from the boom; for his boat was small, and the tide weak, bringing little strain on painter or boom. Besides, this plan was good, for it kept the submarine from bumping the side of the ship—and paint below the water-line is as valuable to a warship as paint above.

Thus moored, the little craft, with only her deck and conning-tower showing, rode lightly at the end of her tether, while Ross and his men—all but one, to watch—climbed aboard and ate their dinner.

Ross finished quickly, and sought the deck; for, on going down to the wardroom, he had seen among the visitors from shore the one girl in the world to him—the girl he had met at Newport, Washington, and New York, whom he wanted as he wanted life, but whom he had not asked for yet, because he had felt so sure of her.

And now this surety was jolted out of his consciousness; for she was there escorted by a man she had often described, and whom Ross recognized from the description—a tall, dark, "captainish"-looking fellow, with a large mustache; but who, far from being a captain or other kind of superman, was merely a photographer—yet a wealthy and successful photographer, whose work was unusual and artistic.

Ross, though an efficient naval officer, was anything but "captainish"; he was simply a clean-shaven, clean-cut young fellow, with a face that mirrored every emotion of his soul. Knowing this infirmity—if such it is—he resolutely put down the jealous thoughts that surged through his brain; and when the visitors, guests of the captain, reached the deck, he met them, and was introduced to Mr. Foster with as pleasant a face as the girl had ever seen.

Then, with the captain's permission, he invited them down to inspect his submarine. A plank from the lower grating of the gangway to the deck of the smaller craft was all that was needed, and along this they went, the girl ahead, supported by Mr. Foster, and Ross following, with a messenger boy from the bridge following him.

At the hatch, the girl paused and shrank back, for the wide-open eyes of the caretaker were looking up at her. Ross surmised this, and called to the man to come up and get his dinner; then, as the man passed him and stepped onto the plank, the messenger got his attention. The officer of the deck desired to speak with him, he said.

Ross explained the manner of descent, admonished his guests to touch nothing until he returned, and followed the messenger back to the officer of the deck. It was nothing of importance, simply a matter pertaining to the afternoon drill; and, somewhat annoyed, Ross returned. But he paused at the end of the plank; a loud voice from below halted him, and he did not care to interrupt. Nor did he care to go back, leaving them alone in a submarine.

"I mean it," Foster was saying vehemently. "I hope this boat does go to the bottom."

"Why, Mr. Foster!" cried the girl. "What a sentiment!"

"I tell you I mean it. You have made life unbearable."

"I make your life unbearable?"

"Yes, you, Irene. You know I have loved you from the beginning. And you have coquetted with me, played with me—as a cat plays with a mouse. When I have endeavored to escape, you have drawn me back by smiles and favor, and given me hope. Then it is coldness and disdain. I am tired of it."

"I am sorry, Mr. Foster, if anything in my attitude has caused such an impression. I have given you no special smiles or favors, no special coldness or disdain."

"But I love you. I want you. I cannot live without you."

"You lived a long time without me, before we met."

"Yes, before we met. Before I fell under the spell of your personality. You have hypnotized me, made yourself necessary to me. I am heartsick all the time, thinking of you."

"Then you must get over it, Mr. Foster. I must think of myself."

"Then you do not care for me, at all?"

"I do, but only as an acquaintance."

"Not even as a friend?"

"I do not like to answer such pointed questions, sir; but, since you ask, I will tell you. I do not like you, even as a friend. You demand so much. You are very selfish, never considering my feelings at all, and you often annoy me with your moods. Frankly, I am happier away from you."

"My moods!" Foster repeated, bitterly. "You cause my moods. But I know what the real trouble is. I was all right until Ross came along."

"You have no right, Mr. Foster," said the girl, angrily, "to bring Lieutenant Ross' name into this discussion."

"Oh, I understand. Do you think he can marry you on his pay?"

"Mr. Ross' pay would not influence him, nor me."

"Well, I'll tell you this"—and Foster's voice became a snarl—"you two won't be married. I'll see to it. I want you; and if I can't have you, no one else shall."

"Whew!" whistled Ross, softly, while he smiled sweetly, and danced a mental jig in the air. Then he danced a few steps of a real jig, to apprise them of his coming. "Time to end this," he said; then called out, cheerily: "Look out below," and entered the hatch.

"Got a bad habit," he said, as he descended, "of coming down this ladder by the run. Must break myself, before I break my neck. Well, how are you making out? Been looking around?"

The girl's face, pale but for two red spots in her cheeks, was turned away from him as he stepped off the ladder, and she trembled visibly. Foster, though flushed and scowling, made a better effort at self-control.

"Why, no, lieutenant," he said, with a sickly smile. "It is all strange and new to us. We were waiting for you. But I have become slightly interested in this—" He indicated a circular window, fixed in the steel side of the boat. "Isn't it a new feature in submarines?"

"Yes, it is," answered Ross. "But it has long been known that glass will stand a stress equal to that of steel, so they've given us deadlights. See the side of the ship out there? We can see objects about twenty feet away near the surface. Deeper down it is darker."

"And I suppose you see some interesting sights under water," pursued Foster, now recovered in poise.

"Yes, very interesting—and some very harrowing. I saw a man drowning not long ago. We were powerless to help him."

"Heavens, what a sight!" exclaimed Foster. "The expression on his face must have been tragic."

"Pitiful—the most pitiful I ever looked at. He seemed to be calling to us. Such agony and despair; but it did not last long."

"But while it *did* last—did you have a camera? What a chance for a photographer! That is my line, you know. Did ever a photographer get a chance to photograph the expression on the face of a drowning man? What a picture it would be?"

"Don't," said the girl, with a shudder. "For mercy's sake, do not speak of such things."

"I beg your pardon, Miss Fleming," said Ross, gently. "It was very tactless in me."

"And I, Miss Fleming," said Foster, with a bow, "was led away by professional enthusiasm. Please accept *my* apology, too. Still, lieutenant, I must say that I would like the chance."

"Sorry, Mr. Foster," answered Ross, coldly. "We do all sorts of things to men in the navy, but we don't drown them for the sake of their pictures. Suppose I show you around, for at two bells the men will be back from their dinner. Now, aft here, is the gasoline engine, which we use to propel the boat on the surface. We can't use it submerged, however, on account of the exhaust; so, for under-water work, we use a strong storage battery to work a motor. You see the motor back there, and under this deck is the storage battery—large jars of sulphuric acid and lead. It is a bad combination if salt water floods it."

"How? What happens?" asked Foster.

"Battery gas, or, in chemical terms, chlorine gas is formed. It is one of the most poisonous and suffocating of all gases. That is the real danger in submarine boats—suffocation from chlorine. It will remain so until we get a better form of motive power, liquid or compressed air, perhaps. And here"—Ross led them to a valve wheel amidships—"as though to invite such disaster, they've given us a sea cock."

"What's it for?" asked Foster.

"To sink the boat in case of fire. It's an inheritance from steamboats—pure precedent—and useless, for a submarine cannot catch fire. Why, a few turns of that wheel when in the awash trim would admit enough water in two minutes to sink the boat. I've applied for permission to abolish it."

"Two minutes, you say. Does it turn easy? Would it be possible to accidentally turn it?"

"Very easy, and very possible. I caution my men every day."

"And in case you do sink, and do not immediately suffocate, how do you rise?"

"By pumping out the water. There's a strong pump connected with that motor aft there, that will force out water against the pressure of the sea at fifty fathoms down. That is ten atmospheres—pretty hard pressure. But, if the motor gets wet, it is useless to work the pump; so, we can be satisfied that, if we sink by means of the sea cock, we stay sunk. There is a hand pump, to use on the surface with dead batteries, but it is useless at any great depth."

"What do you mean by the awash trim, lieutenant?" asked Foster, who was now looking out through the deadlight.

"The diving trim—that is, submerged all but the conning-tower. I'll show you, so that you can say that you have really been under water."

Ross turned a number of valves similar to the sea cock, and the girl's face took on a look of doubt and sudden apprehension.

"You are not going to sink the boat, are you, Mr. Ross?" she asked.

"Oh, no, just filling the tanks. When full, we still have three hundred pounds reserve buoyancy, and would have to go ahead and steer down. But we won't go ahead. Come forward, and I'll show you the torpedo-tube."

Foster remained, moodily staring through the deadlight, while the other two went forward. Ross noticed his abstraction, and, ascribing it to weariness of technical detail, did not press him to follow, and continued his lecture to Miss Fleming in a lower tone and in evident embarrassment.

"Now, here is the tube," he said. "See this rear door. It is water-tight. When a torpedo is in the tube, as it is now, we admit water, as well; and, to expel the torpedo, we only have to open the forward door, apply compressed air, and out it goes. Then it propels and steers itself. We have a theory—no, not a theory now, for it has been proved—that, in case of accident, a submarine's crew can all be ejected through the tube except the last man. He must remain to die, for he cannot eject himself. That man"—Ross smiled and bowed low to the girl—"must be the commander."

"How terrible!" she answered, interested, but looking back abstractedly at Foster. "Why do you remain at this work? Your life is always in danger."

"And on that account promotion is more probable. I want promotion, and more pay"—he lowered his voice and took her hand—"so that I may ask for the love and the life companionship of the dearest and best girl in the world."

She took her gaze off Foster, cast one fleeting glance into the young lieutenant's pleading face, then dropped her eyes to the deck, while her face flushed rosily. But she did not withdraw her hand.

"Must you wait for promotion?" she said, at length.

"No, Irene, no," exclaimed Ross, excitedly, squeezing the small hand in his own. "Not if you say so; but I have nothing but my pay."

"I have always been poor," she said, looking him frankly in the face. "But, John, that is not it. I am afraid. He—Mr. Foster, threatened us—vowed we would never— Oh, and he turned something back there after you started. He did it so quickly—I just barely saw him as I turned to follow you. I do not know what it was. I did not understand what you were describing."

"He turned something! What?"

"It was a wheel of some kind."

Ross looked at Foster. He was now on the conning-tower ladder, half-way up, looking at his opened watch, with a lurid, malevolent twist to his features.

"Say your prayers!" yelled Foster, insanely. "You two are going to die, I say. Die, both of you."

He sprang up the ladder, and Ross bounded aft, somewhat bewildered by the sudden turn of events. He was temporarily at his wits' end. But when Foster floundered down to the deck in a deluge of water from above, and the conning-tower hatch closed with a ringing clang, he understood. One look at the depth indicator was enough. The boat was sinking. He sprang to the sea-cock valve. It was wide open.

"Blast your wretched, black heart and soul," he growled, as he hove the wheel around. "Did you open this valve? Hey, answer me. You did, didn't you? And thought to escape yourself—you coward!"

"Oh, God!" cried Foster, running about distractedly. "We're sinking, and I can't get out."

Ross tightened the valve, and sprang toward him, the murder impulse strong in his soul. In imagination, he felt his fingers on the throat of the other, and every strong muscle of his arms closing more tightly his grip. Then their plight dominated his thoughts; he merely struck out silently, and knocked the photographer down.

"Get up," he commanded, as the prostrate man rolled heavily over on his hands and knees. "Get up, I may need you."

Foster arose, and seated himself on a torpedo amidships, where he sank his head in his hands. With a glance at him, and a reassuring look at the girl, who still remained forward, Ross went aft to connect up the pump. But as he went, he noticed that the deck inclined more and more with each passing moment.

He found the depressed engine room full of water, and the motor flooded. It was useless to start it; it would short-circuit at the first contact; and he halted, wondering at the boat's being down by the stern so much, until a snapping sound from forward apprised him of the reason.

The painter at the boom had held her nose up until the weight was too much for it, and, with its parting, the little craft assumed nearly an even keel, while the water rushed forward among the battery jars beneath the deck. Then a strong, astringent odor arose through the seams in the deck, and Ross became alive.

"Battery gas!" he exclaimed, as he ran amidships, tumbling Foster off the torpedo with a kick—for he was in his way. He reached up and turned valve after valve, admitting compressed air from the flasks to the filled tanks, to blow out the water. This done, he looked at the depth indicator; it registered seventy feet; but, before he could determine the speed of descent, there came a shock that permeated the whole boat. They were on the bottom.

"And Lord only knows," groaned Ross, "how much we've taken in! But it's only three atmospheres, thank God. Here, you," he commanded to the nerveless Foster, who had again found a seat. "Lend a hand on this pump. I'll deal with your case when we get up."

"What must I do?" asked Foster, plaintively, as he turned his face, an ashy green now, toward Ross.

"Pump," yelled Ross, in his ear. "Pump till you break your back if necessary. Ship that brake."

He handed Foster his pump-brake, and they shipped them in the hand-pump. But, heave as they might, they could not move it, except in jerks of about an inch. With an old-fashioned force-pump, rusty from disuse, a three-inch outlet, and three atmospheres of pressure, pumping was useless, and they gave it up, even though the girl added her little weight and strength to the task.

Ross had plenty of compressed air in the numerous air flasks scattered about, and, as he could blow out no more tanks, he expended a jet into the choking atmosphere of the boat. It sweetened the air a little, but there was enough of the powerful, poisonous gas generated to keep them all coughing continually. However, he seated the girl close to the air jet, so that she need not suffer more than was necessary.

"Are we in danger, John?" she asked. "Real danger, I mean?"

"Yes, dear, we are," he answered, tenderly. "And it is best that you should know. I have driven out all the water possible, and we cannot pump at this depth. Higher up we could. But I can eject the torpedo from the tube, and perhaps the others. That will lighten us a good deal."

He went forward, driving Foster before him—for he did not care to leave him too close to the girl—and pushed him bodily into the cramped space between the tube and the trimming tanks.

"Stay there," he said, incisively, "until I want you."

"What can I do?" whimpered the photographer, a brave bully before the girl, when safe; a stricken poltroon now. "I'll do anything you say, to get to the surface."

"You'll get to the surface in time," answered Ross, significantly. "How much do you weigh?"

"Two hundred pounds."

"Two hundred more than we want. However, I'll get rid of this torpedo."

Ross drove the water out of the tube, opened the breech-door; and, reaching in with a long, heavy wire, lifted the starting lever and water tripper that gave motion to the torpedo's engine. The exhaust of air into the tube was driven out into the boat by the rapidly moving screws, and in a few moments the engine ran down.

Then Ross closed the door, flooded the tube, opened the forward door, or port, and sent out the torpedo, confident that, with a dead engine, it would float harmlessly to the surface, and perhaps locate their position to the fleet; for there could be little doubt that the harbor above was dotted with boats, dragging for the sunken submarine.

As the torpedo went out, Ross noticed that the nose of the boat lifted a little, then settled as the tube filled with water. This was encouraging, and he expelled the water. The nose again lifted, but the stern still held to the bottom. There were two other torpedoes, one each side, amidships, and though the dragging to the tube of these heavy weights was a job for all hands, Ross essayed it.

They were mounted on trucks, and with what mechanical aids and purchases he could bring to bear, he and the subdued Foster labored at the task, and in an hour had the starboard torpedo in the tube.

As he was expending weights, he did not take into the 'midship tank an equal weight of water, as was usual to keep the boat in trim, and when the torpedo, robbed of motive power and detonator, went out, the bow lifted still higher, though the stern held, as was evidenced by the grating sound from aft. The tide was drifting the boat along the bottom.

Another hour of hard, perspiring work rid them of the other torpedo, and the boat now inclined at an angle of thirty degrees, down by the stern because of the water in the engine room, but not yet at the critical angle that caused the flooding of the after battery jars as the boat sank.

Ross looked at the depth indicator, but found small comfort. It read off a depth of about sixty feet, but this only meant the lift of the bow. However, the propeller guard only occasionally struck the bottom now, proving to Ross that, could he expend a very little more weight, the boat would rise to the surface, where, even though he might not pump, his periscope and conning-tower could be seen. He panted after his labors until he had regained breath, then said to Foster:

"You next."

"I next? What do you mean?"

"You want to get to the surface, don't you?" said Ross, grimly. "You expressed yourself as willing to do anything I might say, in order to get to the surface. Well, strip off your coat, vest, and shoes, and crawl into that tube."

"What? To drown? No, I will not."

"Yes, you will. Can you swim?"

"I can swim, but not when I am shot out of a gun."

"Then you'll drown. Peel off."

"I cannot. I cannot. Would you kill me?"

"Don't care much," answered Ross, quietly, "if I do. Only I don't want your dead body in the boat. Come, now," he added, his voice rising. "I'm giving you a chance for your life. I can swim, too, and would not hesitate at going out that tube, if I were sure that the boat, deprived of my weight, would rise. But I am not sure, so I send you, not only because you are heavier than I, but because, as Miss Fleming must remain, I prefer to remain, too, to live or die with her. Understand?"

"But, Miss Fleming," cackled Foster. "She can swim. I've heard her say so."

"You cowardly scoundrel," said Ross, his eyes ablaze with scorn and rage. He had already shed his coat and vest. Now he rolled up his shirt-sleeves. "Will you go into that tube of your own volition, conscious, so that you may take a long breath before I flood the tube, or unconscious, and pushed in like a bag of meal, to drown before you know what ails you—which?"

"No," shrieked Foster, as the menacing face and fists of Ross drew close to him. "I will not. Do something else. You are a sailor. You know what to do. Do something else."

Ross' reply was a crashing blow in the face, that sent Foster reeling toward the tube. But he arose, and returned, the animal fear in him changed to courage. He was a powerfully built man, taller, broader, and heavier than Ross, and what he lacked in skill with his fists, he possessed in the momentum of his lunges, and his utter indifference to pain.

Ross was a trained boxer, strong, and agile, and where he struck the larger man he left his mark; but in the contracted floor space of the submarine he was at a disadvantage. But he fought on, striking, ducking, and dodging—striving not only for his own life, but that of the girl whom he loved, who, seated on the 'midship trimming tank, was watching the fight with pale face and wide-open, frightened eyes.

Once, Ross managed to trip him as he lunged, and Foster fell headlong; but before Ross could secure a weapon or implement to aid him in the unequal combat, he was up and coming back, with nose bleeding and swollen, eyes blackened and half closed, and contusions plentifully sprinkled over his whole face.

He growled incoherently; he was reduced by fear and pain to the level of a beast, and, beast-like, he fought for his life—with hands and feet, only the possession of the prehensile thumb, perhaps, preventing him from using his teeth; for Ross, unable to avoid his next blind lunge, went down, with the whole two hundred pounds of Foster on top of him, and felt the stricture of his clutch on his throat.

A man being choked quickly loses power of volition, entirely distinct from the inhibition coming of suppressed breathing; after a few moments, his movements are involuntary.

Ross, with flashes of light before his eyes, soon took his hands from the iron fingers at his throat, and, with the darkening of his faculties, his arms and legs went through flail-like motions, rising and falling, thumping the deck with rhythmic regularity.

Something in this exhibition must have affected the girl at the air jet; for Ross soon began to breathe convulsively, then to see more or less distinctly—while his limbs ceased their flapping—and the first thing he saw was the girl standing over him, her face white as the whites of her distended eyes, her lips pressed tightly together, and poised aloft in her hands one of the pump-brakes, ready for another descent upon the head of Foster, who, still and inert, lay by the side of Ross.

As Ross moved and endeavored to rise, she dropped the club, and sank down, crying his name and kissing him. Then she incontinently fainted.

Ross struggled to his feet, and, though still weak and nerveless, found some spun yarn in a locker, with which he tied the unconscious victim's hands behind his back, and lashed his ankles together. Thus secured, he was harmless when he came to his senses, which happened before Ross had revived the girl. But there were no growling threats coming from him now; conquered and bound, his courage changed to fear again, and he complained and prayed for release.

"Not much," said Ross, busy with the girl. "When I get my wind, I'm going to jam you into that tube, like a dead man. I'll release you inside."

When Miss Fleming was again seated on the tank, breathing fresh air from the jet, Ross went to work with the practical methods of a sailor. He first, by a mighty exercise of all his strength, loaded the frightened Foster on to one of the torpedo trucks, face downward; then he wheeled him to the tube, so that his uplifted face could look squarely into it; then he passed a strap of rope around under his shoulders, to which he applied the big end of a ship's handspike, that happened to be aboard; and to the other end of this, as it lay along the back of Foster, he secured the single block of a small tackle—one of the purchases he had used in handling the torpedoes—and when he had secured the double block to an eyebolt in the bow, he steadied the handspike between his knees, hauled on the fall, with no word to the screaming wretch, and launched him, head and shoulders, into the tube.

As his hands, tied behind him, went in, Ross carefully cut one turn of the spun yarn, hauled away, and as his feet disappeared, he cut the bonds on his ankles; then he advised him to shake his hands and feet clear, pulled out the handspike, slammed the breech-door to, and waited.

The protest from within had never ceased; but at last Ross got from the information, interlarded with pleadings for life, that his hands and feet were free.

"All right. Take a good breath, and I'll flood you," called Ross. "When you're outside, swim up." The voice from within ceased.

Ross threw over the lever that admitted water to the tube, opened the forward door, and applied the compressed air. There was a slight jump to the boat's nose, but with the inrush of water as Foster went out, it sank.

However, when Ross closed the forward door, and had expelled this water, it rose again, and he anxiously inspected the depth indicator.

At first, he hardly dared believe it, but in a few moments he was sure. The indicator was moving, hardly faster than the minute hand of a clock. The boat, released of the last few pounds necessary, was seeking the surface.

"Irene," he shouted, joyously, "we're rising. We'll be afloat before long, and they'll rescue us. Even though we can't pump, they'll see our periscope, and tow us somewhere where they can lift the hatch out of water. It's all over, girl—all over but the shouting. Stand up, and look at the indicator. Only fifty-five feet now."

She stood beside him, supported by his arm, and together they watched the slowly moving indicator. Then Ross casually glanced at the deadlight, and violently forced the girl to her seat.

"Sit still," he commanded, almost harshly. "Sit still, and rest."

For, looking in through the deadlight, was the white face of Foster, washed clean of blood, but filled with the terror and agony of the dying. His hands clutched weakly at the glass, his eyes closed, his mouth opened, and he drifted out of sight.

'Titanic and DeLorean: Belfast's contributions to Time Travel'

by Logan Bruce

The DeLorean car is best known for its role as a time machine in the 1980s film series "Back to the Future". Its appearance in the television show "Chuck" was an homage to those films. Beyond that, little is known about it among the general public. In fact, a leading figure in the Belfast Science Fiction scene once asked (in all seriousness) 'What has DeLorean got to do with Belfast?'

The answer is that, despite being financed by an American millionaire, the factory where the DeLorean cars were manufactured was in Dunmurry, just south of Belfast – within a dozen miles of the shipyard where the Titanic was built.

Also less well-known is the fact that the Titanic itself has been used far more times in time-travel stories than the DeLorean itself!

When the heroic duo in 1960s TV romp "Time Tunnel" take their first leap back in time they end up aboard the RMS Titanic. The Titanic as portrayed in "A Night to Remember", that is.

Back in the 1960s, the production company that made this show held the rights to an enormous back-catalogue of films. Home cinema had not been invented (except for 16mm cine films), and at the time there was no way of exploiting this back-list to its full extent. It was another two decades before VHS was in every home and it became a reasonable business proposition to release classic films on video. So stock footage was taken from classic films and inserted into TV shows to make them seem to have a bigger budget. Only in retrospect can we see how cheap this seems. This technique was used up to the Eighties, most blatantly in the show "MacGyver". British audiences will never forget the car chase from the original "Italian Job" being used to depict Richard Dean Anderson escaping from a Warsaw Pact police force.

Decades later the title characters in the film "Time Bandits" step through a rip in space-time, and find themselves aboard an Edwardian cruise-liner. They bribe their way into the luxurious first class accommodations, and pass themselves off as eccentric millionaires. But when one of them makes the mistake of ordering a drink with plenty of ice ... they end up in the ocean, clinging to a life-ring with the ship's name 'Titanic' emblazoned across it.

The most successful time-travel series of the 1980s is based on the film "Terminator". So far it has produced three film sequels, a television show that ran for two seasons, and many comic-book spin-offs and crossovers. None of them have featured the DeLorean or the Titanic. However, the writer-director James Cameron created the most famous film about the Titanic, named after the ship itself. In all fairness, it has been suggested by those who are not fond of the film that it could also be called 'An old lady ignores her wonderful life and fixates on a one-night stand with a homeless bum'.

It should also be noted that Cameron appears to have based both "Terminator" and "Titanic" on the 1981 film "Somewhere In Time" about time-travel to the Edwardian age and a romance between an American hero and an English damsel. It is best-known these days for pairing Bond girl Jane Seymour with Superman Christopher Reeve, which led to them both getting cameo appearances as members of the Veritas conspiracy in the television show "Smallville".

Jane Seymour's on-screen son in "Smallville", the actor Jensen Ackles, later found fame of his own in the US TV show "Supernatural". When the show's stories examined possible ways to change history, Ackles' character makes a pop-culture reference to DeLorean cars. However, when a character deliberately changes history, all he has to do is stop the Titanic from sinking ...

The greatest fictional time-traveller, the Time Lord known as The Doctor (in UK TV show "Doctor Who") may not have visited the actual Titanic in any television episode, but he DID in one of the radio plays. The title of that story was, of course, 'The Wreck of the Titan'!

There was a Doctor Who Christmas special ("Voyage of the Damned") set aboard the Starship Titanic. The Starship Titanic was also used in an episode of Futurama, and was mentioned in the "Hitch-Hiker's Guide to the Galaxy" series of novels. This last reference led to a video game and a spin-off novel.

Other franchises also have Titanic links. Obi-Wan Kenobi in "Star Wars" had no truck with earth-bound events, but Sir Alec Guinness had a cameo in "Raise the Titanic". And in "Ghostbusters 2", the Titanic (and the ghosts of everyone who died aboard it) actually made it to New York.

But how can one justify, within the logic of a time-travel story, the fact that sooner or later every time-traveller seems to end up aboard the Titanic?

The film "The Time-Traveller's Wife", based on the novel of the same name, mentions that the traveller automatically defaults to visiting "important events". In his case they are merely of personal importance to himself. But on a macro level, this could include events of enormous scale.

Other time-travel black-spots may exist. Most time-travel in fiction seems to involve the latter half of the Twentieth Century. For example, Dr Sam Beckett in "Quantum Leap" can only leap into his own past, allowing him to relive the baby-boomer experience of the 1960s. And much like the Police procedural show "Cold Case", this allows him to take revenge on anything and anyone that offends his modern sensibilities.

But the 51st Century also seems to be a black-spot for time-travellers. In "Doctor Who", both K-9 and the character who uses the alias Captain Jack Harkness are from around the year 5,000 CE.

So we should ask ourselves, was "Time Bandits" right? Could there be a rip in the fabric of the space-time continuum that makes time-travelers land aboard the Titanic with such frequency?

In a Science Fiction universe we could extrapolate that some decisions are so bad that they cause a rip in space-time itself ...

Perhaps the universe tears itself open in an effort to cleanse itself and heal - with the help of time-travellers, of course. So reality itself tries to rewind time, attracting Quantum Leapers to rewrite history in a different direction.

'An Ulsterman among the Icebergs'

by Logan Bruce

In the town of Comber, County Down, there stands a memorial to Thomas Andrews - the man who designed the Titanic. But only twenty-six miles away in the town of Banbridge stands a similar memorial to one of the most outstanding but forgotten members of the brotherhood of Arctic explorers. The heroic sacrifice of Scott, the endurance of Shackleton, the triumph of Amundsen, these are the explorers best remembered. But outside of his hometown, Captain Francis Crozier is a little-known figure of history.

Francis Rawdon Moira Crozier joined the Royal Navy while still a child, in the years after Nelson's victory at Cape Trafalgar. He joined his first ship not at Belfast, near his home, but at Cork - hundreds of miles away, on the southern tip of Ireland. It is a fact whitewashed out of history that a third of the sailors who served aboard Royal Navy ships during the Napoleonic war were from the island of Ireland, for in those days it was still an equal part of the British homeland.

The aftermath of Napoleon's defeat at Waterloo meant that the British Empire's Army and Navy, boosted to massive scale during the war, were drastically cut. A hundred thousand sailors were dumped back on the streets from which they had been press-ganged. But the Post-Napoleonic period also saw a drive towards Imperial expansion. The teenage Crozier set sail for the Pacific Ocean, on the other side of the world.

Crozier's vessel, like every other ship of its day, could only travel from the North Atlantic to the Pacific by sailing round Cape Horn, with all the dangers this entailed. HMS Beagle had yet to chart the rugged coastline of Tierra Del Fuego, never mind deliver Charles Darwin to the Galapagos islands. The lighthouse depicted by Jules Verne was truly 'The Light At The Edge Of the World'.

One Pacific island that Crozier visited was Pitcairn, where he met the last surviving mutineer from HMS Bounty. A quarter of a century earlier the Bounty's crew had forced Captain Bligh and his officers into a long-boat, and cast them adrift. The mutineers then secretly sailed into a secluded exile in the remote and uncharted Pitcairn island. Bligh, in an open-topped boat, navigated his way to safety on a journey that lasted 47 days and covered an estimated 3600 miles. Such an epic feat was the kind of thing that young Crozier was trained to emulate.

Crozier worked his way up through the ranks of the Royal Navy, and in 1839 was given command of HMS Terror. As second-in-command in an expedition led by James Clark Ross (Captain of HMS Erebus) he explored the coast of Antarctica.

In 1845 Crozier, by then a veteran explorer, joined Sir John Franklin's expedition to the northern coast of Canada. Their goal was to discover the North-West Passage to the Indies.

The Indies had been Christopher Columbus' goal when he set sail in 1492, but he had no idea that the American continents blocked his path. Within a century of Columbus' historic voyage, the Eastern coast of North America had been explored by Tudor seamen like John Cabot (born Giovanni Cabotti), Martin Frobisher and Henry

Hudson (after whom the Hudson river and Hudson Bay are both named). But what they really needed was a passage to the Indies, a route that would by-pass the Americas and take them directly to the spice-rich lands of Asia.

By 1845, when Crozier joined Franklin's expedition, spices were of less importance. Whaling, carried out to provide oil for industrial processes and domestic use, was where money could be made. As a result, whaling ships sailed to the most distant parts of the map, and beyond. The Franklin expedition's ice-masters - Reid (aboard the Erebus) and Blanky (on the Terror) - had sailed with whaling fleets from Peterhead, Scotland.

That very year, Herman Melville was still hard on the semi-biographical epic 'Moby Dick'. While Melville himself had never been aboard a ship while it was sunk by an enraged sperm whale, he had met men who had - survivors of the Nantucket whaler Essex. But the whale's onslaught had been the least of their perils, for once the Essex was sunk the whale departed from the scene. The survivors numbered twenty men aboard three open-topped boats in the vast Pacific ocean. By the time they had sailed to within sight of friendly sails, four thousand miles later, they had resorted first to cannibalism of their dead, and then to drawing lots. They sailed farther than Captain Bligh or Shackleton, though the grisly method of their survival is perhaps the reason for their obscurity.

With such risks a constant hazard on long sea voyages, the idea of a shortcut between the Atlantic and Pacific Oceans was an inviting prospect. While the American trans-continental railroad had yet to be constructed, there was still an overland route from the

Mississippi to the California territory. And after the gold strike of 1848 came the surge of gold-hungry immigrants known now as the Forty-niners. But the wagon trails were perilous, as we see from the fate of the infamous Donner Party which mirrored that of the crew of the Essex.

The only alternatives would be the as-then unthinkable industrial projects of creating either a trans-continental railroad connecting the East Coast of the United States with the California territory ... or creating a canal in Panama, where the Americas were at their narrowest.

The Tudor privateer Sir Francis Drake had lost a lot of men along the mule track across the Isthmus of Panama in the 1590s. But even in Crozier's time, centuries later, the building of an industrialised shortcut across the Americas was just as unthinkable. Decades later the Frenchmen who had completed the Suez canal turned their attentions to Panama, but still to no avail. It was only in the Twentieth Century, with the internal combustion engine and the financial might of the United States Government, that the Panama Canal could become a reality.

In Crozier's day, an age of hardships aboard a whaling ship rounding the Horn or on the open prairies taking the tortuous overland route, the bravery of the polar explorers still put them head and shoulders above even their hardiest their contemporaries. But we should not forget that there were already human societies living in the Arctic, and that it was not altogether a wilderness.

In the Nineteenth Century, European officers like Crozier usually treated members of pre-Industrial societies as if they were children. As a result the Europeans did not bother to learn the natives' survival skills, which had been honed over hundreds of generations. Instead the explorers relied on keeping their ships well-stocked with rations. This naturally created further problems. To have enough supplies, a ship would need to stick to deep water. And for an exploration mission into unsurveyed waters, with uncharted reefs and shallows, this was a disaster waiting to happen. Worse, once the ship was lost (with all supplies aboard) there was no back-up plan. In this one can draw a parallel with the Titanic, insofar as the planning was based on the presumed unsinkability of the ship. In neither case was any real thought given to any form of back-up plan.

As it turned out, the Admiralty's contract for the Franklin Expedition's meat provisions went to the lowest bidder. Since quality control inspections were insufficiently thorough, the meat on the Erebus and Terror was diseased. Almost as bad, their measures to prevent outbreaks of scurvy were also inadequate. So the mission would have run into trouble eventually, even if the murderous Arctic conditions had not been a factor.

So Crozier and Franklin, with inadequate provisions and no other means of support, sailed into the Arctic circle ...

When their ships became ice-bound, their supplies exhausted or inedible, Franklin was among the first to perish. Crozier was left in command of over a hundred survivors. Isolated and starving, like the marooned sailors and snowbound settlers before them, they relied on Crozier's leadership and courage.

Two years after last contact with the expedition, a Royal Navy flotilla attempted to rescue Crozier and the other survivors.

This group included a fellow Irish officer in the Royal Navy, Robert McClure. The rescuers searched in vain for any sign of the survivors, but were unable to locate them and eventually had to return to safer waters. But the Royal Navy was not deterred. In 1850 McClure sailed round Cape Horn and into the Pacific Ocean, to attempt the North-West Passage from the Western approach.

Let us pause to examine how undeveloped the western seaboard of the North American continent was. The settlement today known as Seattle was not even founded until 1851, when a group of white settlers sailed up the coast and made their camp on a mud-flat.

Eventually McClure entered the Arctic Ocean via the Bering Strait. His ship was stocked with 3 years worth of provisions, which was later supplemented with wild game shot on Banks' Island. Also, unlike Franklin and Crozier, McClure had an Inuit interpreter among his crew. These preparations, so lacking in the Franklin Expedition, proved useful. He also left messages in cairns for other search parties to track his progress.

Finally, after three years trapped in the ice, McClure succeeded where Crozier and Franklin had not. The message cairns led a search party to make contact with him. McClure and his crew abandoned their ship to the ice, then man-hauled their supplies to the rescue ships which had sailed along Crozier's route into the Passage from the Eastern end. Thus McClure became not only the first explorer to cross the North-West Passage, but also the first to encircle the Americas.

Despite McClure's success, the body of Francis Crozier was never recovered. Years later, Inuit travelers would bring tales of him struggling through the wilderness with an ever-dwindling band of survivors in tow, until Crozier himself was the last man standing.

Fifty years later, Norwegian explorer Roald Amundsen led another expedition to successfully traverse the North-West Passage. This expedition took three years, from 1903 to 1906, and was the first to complete the passage entirely by boat. In contrast with his rivals, Amundsen succeeded because he learned from the Inuit peoples he encountered. Afterwards, Amundsen turned his attentions to Crozier's other great area of exploration – Antarctica.

But McClure was not the only Irish Briton to follow in Crozier's footsteps. Ernest Shackleton, portrayed on the small screen in 2002 by Belfast actor Kenneth Branagh, was a contemporary and rival of Amundsen. Shackleton's great feat was to keep his entire crew alive while marooned in the Antarctic, and then sail 800 miles in an open-topped boat to fetch a rescue party from the island of South Georgia.

Another Irish Briton in the tradition Crozier began was SAS commander Blair Mayne (from County Down, like Crozier himself). In the aftermath of the Second World War, when the military's elite units were being disbanded, Mayne transferred to the British Antarctic Survey in South Georgia.

Mayne had competition, but not from the Norwegians. During the post-war period the USA also sent an expedition, commanded by veteran explorer Rear Admiral Richard E. Byrd, USN. His previous 1932 expedition had inspired HP Lovecraft's sci-fi/horror story "At the Mountains of Madness", notable to Ulster folk for its reference to the Giant's Causeway.

But the most infamous explorer to follow in Crozier's footsteps was Shackleton's contemporary, and Amundsen's greatest rival, the English explorer Robert Scott. In 1911 Scott and his team surveyed Cape Crozier on the most easterly point of Ross Island in Antarctica. The Cape had been discovered in 1841 when Crozier was second-in-command of James Clark Ross's expedition with HMS Erebus and HMS Terror. The names of the ships were assigned to two of the highest peaks, while the Cape itself was named after Francis Crozier, captain of HMS Terror.

Months later, Scott and his men set out on their fateful expedition to the South Pole. When they reached it they found that Amundsen's team had beaten them by a matter of days. On their way home, Scott and his companions all met the same bitter end that Crozier and his crew had suffered.

In a last bitter irony, Scott's last diary entry was dated 29 March 1912. Just a fortnight later, Crozier's countryman Thomas Andrews and over a thousand other souls perished when the Titanic met her own infamous fate.

Bibliography:
Captain Francis Crozier – Last Man Standing?
Smith, Michael (2006).
Cork, Ireland: Collins Press.
ISBN 1905172095

'If—' by Rudyard Kipling

If you can keep your head when all about you
Are losing theirs and blaming it on you;
If you can trust yourself when all men doubt you,
But make allowance for their doubting too:
If you can wait and not be tired by waiting,
Or being lied about, don't deal in lies,
Or being hated don't give way to hating,
And yet don't look too good, nor talk too wise;

If you can dream—and not make dreams your master;
If you can think—and not make thoughts your aim,
If you can meet with Triumph and Disaster
And treat those two impostors just the same:
If you can bear to hear the truth you've spoken
Twisted by knaves to make a trap for fools,
Or watch the things you gave your life to, broken,
And stoop and build 'em up with worn-out tools;

If you can make one heap of all your winnings
And risk it on one turn of pitch-and-toss,
And lose, and start again at your beginnings
And never breathe a word about your loss:
If you can force your heart and nerve and sinew

To serve your turn long after they are gone,
And so hold on when there is nothing in you
Except the Will which says to them: 'Hold on!'

If you can talk with crowds and keep your virtue,
Or walk with Kings—nor lose the common touch,
If neither foes nor loving friends can hurt you,
If all men count with you, but none too much:
If you can fill the unforgiving minute
With sixty seconds' worth of distance run,
Yours is the Earth and everything that's in it,
And—which is more—you'll be a Man, my son!

'First Crossing of the Atlantic?'

by Logan Bruce

The Titanic, like the Titan in the preceding novella, sank while crossing the Atlantic ocean. By the age of steam-power, this was one of the world's main trading routes. But exactly who was the first sailor to use that route? There have been many candidates proposed as the first European to discover the Americas, long before the time of Columbus.

Henry Sinclair, a Scottish nobleman, is said to have sailed across the Atlantic a full century before Columbus set sail. It is possible he could have sailed part of the way, at least. He could certainly have travelled to the Norse settlements on Iceland and Greenland, and if he had a crew willing to sail further then it is a definite possibility.

But even if Henry did sail to the Americas, he was only following the route of the Viking explorers. Erik the Red had been exiled to Iceland, and his son Leif Eriksson explored even further to the west. A Viking longhouse has been uncovered in Newfoundland, though it is more likely site of a winter stay than an attempt at long-term settlement.

But even before the Vikings crossed the Atlantic, we have tales of the mythical Great Voyage.

The Great Voyage has been much neglected by modern

Fantasy literature. The one example that readers would be most familiar with is the book "Voyage of the Dawn Treader" by CS Lewis. Of course, Lewis was originally from Ulster and thus the inspiration of many aspects of the Narnia series come from the legends of his homeland.

The Great Voyage is a staple of ancient myths and legends. In Greek mythology there is the Odyssey, a fictionalised account of the Greek return from the Trojan wars. Ancient Rome added the Aeneid to that series, creating a fictionalised voyage around the Mediterranean until the scene was set for the eventual founding of Rome itself. In contrast with these fictionalised accounts, there may actually be a basis of truth in the story of Jason and the Argonauts. The golden fleece they sought may be a reference to the Scythians of the Caucasus region, who used woolen fleeces to sieve gold-dust from the mountain streams.

In Irish mythology the Great Voyage is generally associated with a monk named Brendan, commonly referred to as Brendan the Voyager. He is said to have sailed past a number of islands, travelling ever westward. However, the more reliable historical accounts do not link Brendan to sea travel at all. He was a contemporary of Comgal, the Abbot of Bangor Abbey and a rival of Columba (also known as Colm O'Neill). So how did Brendan become known as The Voyager?

The early Christian Church in Ireland tended to incorporate historical Pagan myths and legends into their own mythology. Deeds done by great Kings and Druids were later attributed to Christian Missionaries, referred to as "Saints". Druids cast spells, which apparently made them evil, while a so-called Saint could say a prayer and achieve magic through the same means.

The story of Brendan the Voyager is preceded by an even older tale, that of the similarly-named Bran the Voyager. Bran was a Pagan King, and it seems no small leap that he was written out of history by Christians who attributed his great deeds to one of their missionaries who had a similar-sounding name.

But what evidence is there of a historical King Bran?

Columba, contemporary of Brendan, served at the court of the Ulster-Scots King Aedan Mac Gabran. Aedan ruled Dal Riada, a Kingdom which spanned the Irish Sea and stretched from the river Bann in Ulster to deep inside Scotland. We might deduce that King Bran was in fact a corruption of the name Gabran, Aedan's predecessor as King of Dal Riada.

Aedan Mac Gabran has one other famous relative. In the annals of Columba it is written that Aedan had a nephew named Artur, who died in battle at Camboglann. This is the closest match to a historical King Arthur that has yet been discovered. And if King Bran had sailed across the Atlantic, island-hopping as later Vikings would, he would surely have brought his kinsmen with him. Perhaps the first European feet to set foot on the Americas belonged to Artur himself.

'Which Titan is TitanCon named after?' by Logan Bruce

For some reason this is the one question that interviewers love to ask the Convention Directors of Belfast's TitanCon during interviews.

The automatic association with Belfast is the Titanic, especially during the centenary period. After all, it was the largest moving man-made object in the world during its brief existence.

The cranes "Samson" and "Goliath", towering over the Titanic's birthplace at Harland & Wolff shipyards like twin Collossi of Rhodes, also add to Belfast's reputation as a city of Titans. By strange coincidence, "Samson and Goliath" was the name of a 1960s cartoon show about a magical superhero and his pet – a cartoon that was plundered for ideas by "He-Man and the Masters of the Universe" (which was based on a series of action figures designed as spin-off merchandise to the film "Conan the Barbarian").

However, Ulster's place as the Land of Titans is not limited to the industrial wonders of the Twentieth Century. To start with, we should look at the original press release announcing TitanCon 2011 to the media:

Northern Ireland, home of "Gulliver's Travels" and the "Chronicles of Narnia", is recovering its status as world capital of Fantasy fiction thanks to "Your Highness" and "Game of Thrones". The Swords & Sorcery genre will finally come home to Ulster, land of Titans, this September at TitanCon 2011!

Ireland in general, and Ulster in particular, has a long traditional association with Fantasy fiction. Ancient Irish myths like Finn McCool and legends such as the Ulster Cycle have influenced modern Fantasy tales. For example, Robert E Howard named his most famous hero after Conan of the Fianna. Jonathan Swift lived near Belfast, and it has been suggested that the image of Lemuel Gulliver pegged down by Lilliputians was inspired by a local geographical feature now known as "Napoleon's Nose". CS Lewis was inspired by Northern Ireland, and particularly the Mourne Mountains, to create his fictional realm of Narnia. And in recent years, Ulster has played home to Fantasy extravaganzas 'Your Highness' and 'Game of Thrones' (just renewed for a second year's filming).

This all makes Belfast the natural home for TitanCon - Northern Ireland's science fiction and fantasy literature, media and gaming convention. The jam-packed schedule includes discussion panels on HBO and George RR Martin's 'Game of Thrones'. The

event is organised and run by the Brotherhood Without Banners
(George RR Martin's fangroup), Studio NI (Northern Ireland's
largest arts and culture group) and The Other Ones (a Belfast
science fiction and fantasy society).

---- END

Yes, the Cave Hill Titan is listed as an inspiration for scenes in Swift's
"Gulliver's Travels" and Lewis' Narnia book "The Silver Chair". Even
Finn McCool and Conan get a mention.

The Cave Hill Titan is a staple of Fantasy fiction – it even
makes an appearance of sorts in Terry Pratchett's "The Light
Fantastic", the second Discworld novel. It was filmed under the title
"Colour of Magic", somewhat misleadingly because this was in fact
the title of the FIRST book. In the relevant scene, Rincewind (David
Jason), Twoflower (Sean Astin) and Herrena the Henna-Haired
Harridan (Liz May Brice) shelter in a cave. Or at least, what they
THINK is a cave. The result is reminiscent of a certain scene in "The
Empire Strikes Back".

But as the press release makes clear, this is not the only
gigantic figure associated with Ulster's mythology. Finn McCool is a
figure associated with the construction of the Giant's Causeway, one
of the most famous geographical features in the world. The story is
that Finn built the Causeway so he could cross over to Scotland and
fight a Scottish giant. But when he first laid eyes on the Scottish

giant, and realised that the Scot was even larger and stronger than himself, he fled home. The Scotsman pursued him across the Causeway, so Finn hid in his baby's crib. When the Scots Titan looked into the crib and saw what he though was the baby, he assumed its father would be completely massive in comparison. The Scotsman fled, tearing up the Causeway as he went, which explains its current incomplete state.

The character of Finn McCool is well known in Northern Ireland and is commonly used in local advertising. For example, the Belfast ice-hockey team is called the Belfast Giants, and their logo depicts the enormous figure of Finn McCool standing over it the team's name.

But not everyone thinks of Belfast when they hear the word Titan.

'You're going to hold a SciFi convention on the surface of Titan, the moon of Saturn?'

This was the question, aimed in jest, that the TitanCon crew were asked more than once at the World Science Fiction Convention 2011 in Reno, Nevada. The moon named Titan had recently been mentioned in the US SyFy channel TV show 'Eureka', so small wonder so many fans made that association.

In the Judge Dredd universe, set 122 years in our future, Titan is also home to the most secure prison in the solar system.

The moon was named after the monsters of Greek mythology, made familiar to the modern public in the film 'Clash of the Titans'. And in the recent 3-D remake, Ulsterman Liam Neeson played the father-god Zeus. Previously, Neeson had played a different father-god: Aslan in the Narnia series, written by his fellow Ulsterman CS Lewis.

The truth is, "Titan" is a generic term in Fantasy fiction these days. Even in the Song of Ice and Fire/Game of Thrones series there is reference to the "Titan of Braavos", their world's equivalent of the Colossus of Rhodes.

The bottom line is, TitanCon is a great name for a Convention because it works on so many levels.

What caused the sinking of the Titanic?
by S R Logan

Water, H_2O, is a highly unusual compound in that as the temperature is decreased, and the liquid state freezes to become a solid, an expansion occurs. This means, of course, that the solid formed, ice, has a lower density than the liquid. Far from being an idle curiosity, this behaviour means that ice floats on water. Not only do ice cubes float at the surface of your orange squash but icebergs float in the sea.

In a liquid there are usually various attractive forces between molecules and the existence of these forces serves to hold the molecules together so that we have the liquid state rather than a gas. As the temperature is lowered, a point is reached where the motion of individual molecules has been constrained by these weakly attractive forces. Thus cooling the liquid causes crystals to be formed, of a type called molecular crystals, in which the individual molecules are held close together in a regular array, occupying less volume than would the same molecules when they are all moving around independently in the liquid state. So in forming such crystals a contraction occurs and the crystals have a higher density than the liquid. The inter-molecular forces of the above type are called Van der Waals forces, after the name of a nineteenth century Dutch physicist.

In some compounds, the molecules are capable of inter-molecular interactions of a type quite different from Van der Waals forces. If the smallest atom, hydrogen (H), is bonded to an atom, X, which is both small and highly electronegative, then there can be substantial attractive forces between the H atom of one molecule and this small and highly electronegative atom X of another molecule. So in addition to the normal covalent bonds formed by each atom, we may also have a special bond between these two atoms, H and X. In this way two or perhaps more of the molecules may (perhaps temporarily) be joined together. This additional mode of interaction is known as the hydrogen bond, and it is usually denoted by a dotted line whereas a full line is used to denote a much stronger covalent bond.

$$— H - - - - X$$

The best candidates for the small highly electronegative atom X are fluorine (F), oxygen (O), and nitrogen (N). In one sense, fluorine is best because it forms the strongest hydrogen bonds, but with fluorine being univalent the consequences are not correspondingly striking. Divalent oxygen is only a little less electronegative and it provides an easy illustration of the effects of hydrogen bonding.

Let us look at the compounds H—O—H (water), CH_3—O—H (methanol) and CH_3—O—CH_3 (dimethyl ether), where the H atoms of the water molecule are being replaced, one at a time, by methyl groups, that is by a carbon atom with three H atoms bonded to it. One consequence is that the molecular weight increases in steps of 14, so that for these three compounds they are 18; 32; 46. Whereas for molecules of a single type (such as the alkanes of general formula

C_nH_{2n+2}) the boiling point increases with increasing molecular weight, for our series the boiling points decrease: 100 °C for water, 65 °C for methanol and -23 °C for dimethyl ether.

This trend is readily explained by invoking hydrogen bonding. Water, H_2O, is a compound with very strong hydrogen bonding between molecules, a fact which must cause considerable elevation of the temperature needed to cause the molecules to leave the liquid phase and go, individually, into the vapour phase. Note that each water molecule has two H atoms that can form hydrogen bonds with the O atoms of other molecules. By contrast, dimethyl ether has no H atoms bonded to O atoms and is thus incapable of forming hydrogen bonds, so it is a gas at ambient temperatures. Methanol lies in between in regard to both its molecular weight and its boiling point. It can engage in hydrogen bonding but to a lesser extent than water in that it has only one H atom per molecule that is capable of so doing.

To show the relevance, we must look in some detail at the structure of ice. When molecules of water come together to form a crystalline state the only significant forces involved are those of hydrogen bonding. In water the three atoms are not collinear but have an angle, H---O---H, of 104.5°. This value is not far from the tetrahedral angle of 109.5°, where a regular tetrahedron is a three-dimensional structure with 4 flat sides and 4 corners, and the angle in question is that between any pair of lines between the centre of the tetrahedron and one of the corners.

The issue of how the extra-nuclear electrons participate in forming covalent bonds is an extensive one, mostly of marginal relevance to the current theme. One of the applicable theories sees the valence orbitals of the oxygen atom, that is the 2s and the 2p orbitals, as being used to generate four equivalent atomic orbitals, all of equal energy. These orbitals project in four different directions, namely towards the corners of a regular tetrahedron. The O atom has 6 valence electrons so we assign two electrons to each of two of these equivalent orbitals, and one each to the other two. The formation of a covalent bond requires the pairing of two electrons from different atoms, so towards each of these two latter orbitals we bring up a hydrogen atom with its 1s electron, and in this way the two covalent bonds, O---H, are formed. However, our tetrahedron will not now be quite symmetrical in that where an equivalent orbital projects toward the H atom we have a bonding pair and an H atom nucleus, and where we have no H atom we just have the non-bonding pair of electrons, commonly called a lone pair. The mutual repulsion between the two lone pairs will be greater than that between a lone pair and a bonding pair, which will be greater than that between the two bonding pairs. Consequently we would expect that the separation of the bonding pairs would be a little less than the tetrahedral angle and the experimental value of 104.5° is consistent with this rationalisation.

We now have the basis on which we may proceed to the structure of crystalline ice. Starting with a molecule of water, where the two O---H bonds and the two lone pairs constitute an almost tetrahedral structure, let us locate it with the two O---H groups pointing up and the two lone pairs pointing down, as in the centre of Figure 1. We deem that a hydrogen bond is formed when we align the O—H group of one water molecule with one of the lone pairs of another water molecule. Thus each O—H group of the central water molecule can interact with a lone pair of a water molecule above it, and each lone pair of the central molecule may engage with an O—H group of another water molecule below it, as in Figure 1. In this way, our central water molecule is hydrogen bonded to **four** other water molecules. On reflection there is nothing unique about this central molecule, save that we have chosen to put it under the spotlight. Every water molecule in the interior of an ice crystal will have the same role, and will be held in place by four hydrogen bonds, arranged almost tetrahedrally.

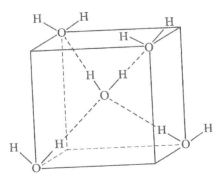

Figure 1: an illustration of the crystalline structure of ice, where each H_2O molecule is hydrogen bonded with four others, arranged almost tetrahedrally.

But whereas a water molecule in ice has only 4 nearest neighbours, some metals (such as copper or nickel) crystallise in a close packed arrangement where each atom has 12 nearest neighbours. Some harder metals (such as tungsten or iron) have a crystal structure where every atom has 8 nearest neighbours. With all these metals the liquid state undergoes a decrease in volume as it solidifies, because of the relatively close packing of the atoms in the crystal. The reason for the expansion of water as it freezes is then apparent; it is a consequence of the crystal structure, with each molecule having only 4 nearest neighbours. This, in a nutshell, is the reason ice floats on water. The hydrogen bonding which holds ice together imposes on it a relatively open crystal structure of inherently low density.

Returning to the bonding theory invoked above in regard to the oxygen atom, let us apply the same process to an atom of carbon (C).. From the 2s and the 2p orbitals we may generate four equivalent atomic orbitals, all of equal energy, and pointing towards the corners of a regular tetrahedron. A carbon atom has four valence electrons so we assign one to each orbital. Let us then bring four similar carbon atoms around this central C atom and as the respective atomic orbitals overlap, let the two electrons, one from each atom, pair off to form a covalent bond. Continuing this process will build up a three-dimensional structure in which each C atom is covalently bonded to four other C atoms disposed tetrahedrally around it. This is the structure of diamond, and diamond (as well as being a girl's best friend) is the hardest material known, with no real rivals.

Ice has a crystal structure differing only slightly from that of diamond, so it also is endowed with considerable hardness and strength in all three dimensions. The strength of a hydrogen bond between two molecules of water is perhaps 0.1 times that of the covalent single bond between two carbon atoms, but ten percent of the extreme degree of hardness of diamond is enough to be taken seriously and sufficient to cause untold damage.

To sum up, why did the Titanic meet its doom on the fateful night of 14 April, 1912? It may all be seen as an unhappy consequence of hydrogen bonding. On account of its hydrogen bonded structure ice has a low density and floats on water, so the icebergs were lying in wait on the surface of the sea, ready for any ship guided by the unwary. Also icebergs, made of crystalline ice, are very hard, for the reason that all the water molecules within them are rigidly held together by hydrogen bonding.

The above is an expanded and free-standing version of a comment in a recent textbook of physical chemistry.
See "Physical Chemistry for the Biomedical Sciences",
by S R Logan; Taylor & Francis, London; 1998, p.90.

Blood of Thrones
by Logan Bruce

It was a time of civil war ...

From the days of MacBeth, last great Keltic King of Scotland ...

To the wars of Edgar the Aethling, the last Saxon King of England ...

From the Pagan standing stones of Myrrdin the Druid ...

To the gates of Jerusalem itself ...

Ancient Bloodlines battle for the Thrones of Britannia!

"Blood of Thrones" is a historical/fantasy novel set around the time of the Norman conquest of England and the First Crusade. The title is a reference to Kurosawa's film "Throne of Blood". As this may suggest, the historical figure of MacBeth is a central character in the story. The action crosses over half a century, as secret societies plot against each other in 11th Century Europe.

"... a breathtaking ride, a very broad canvas ..."
Dr Steve Flanders, School of History at Queen's University Belfast

The book was written according to strict rules - only 30 days to write, 30 days to edit. It is now in print thanks to Speculative Fiction publisher "The ORB". For every copy sold, 20% (£1) of the £5 cover-price goes to the charity nominated by Studio NI, the largest Arts and Culture Group in the North of Ireland. At time of publication, the nominated charity is Action Cancer (Charity reg no. XN 48533).

Copies can be ordered on-line from Amazon at
http://www.orb-store.com/blood.htm

Donations can be made directly to Action Cancer at
http://www.justgiving.com/orbzine

TITANIA: Top Independent Talented Artistes of Northern Ireland (Volumes 1-3)

Studio NI has published an omnibus edition containing its first three anthologies of ghost stories and work of a supernatural nature.

For every copy sold, 20% of the cover-price goes to the charity nominated by Studio NI, the largest Arts and Culture Group in the North of Ireland. At time of publication, the nominated charity is Action Cancer (Charity reg no. XN 48533).

More information at:
http://www.TitanFest.com

Milton Keynes UK
Ingram Content Group UK Ltd.
UKHW021354220424
441558UK00008B/447

9 781907 572067